SWEET & BITTER RIVALS

Also by Jessica Burkhart

THE SADDLEHILL ACADEMY SERIES
The Showdown

THE CANTERWOOD CREST SERIES

For older readers
Life Inside My Mind

For younger readers
THE UNICORN MAGIC SERIES

Saddlehill Academy

SWEET & BITTER RIVALS

JESSICA BURKHART

Aladdin

New York   London   Toronto   Sydney   New Delhi

This book is a work of fiction. Any references to historical events, real people, or real places are used fictitiously. Other names, characters, places, and events are products of the author's imagination, and any resemblance to actual events or places or persons, living or dead, is entirely coincidental.

An imprint of Simon & Schuster Children's Publishing Division
1230 Avenue of the Americas, New York, New York 10020
First Aladdin paperback edition May 2023
Text copyright © 2023 by Jessica Burkhart
Cover illustration copyright © 2023 by Lana Dudarenko
Cover filigree and crest by ProVectors/iStock
Cover horses by SvetlanaSoloveva/iStock
Also available in an Aladdin hardcover edition.
All rights reserved, including the right of reproduction in whole or in part in any form.
ALADDIN and related logo are registered trademarks of Simon & Schuster, Inc.
For information about special discounts for bulk purchases, please contact
Simon & Schuster Special Sales at 1-866-506-1949 or business@simonandschuster.com.
The Simon & Schuster Speakers Bureau can bring authors to your live event.
For more information or to book an event contact the Simon & Schuster Speakers Bureau
at 1-866-248-3049 or visit our website at www.simonspeakers.com.
Cover designed by Karin Paprocki
Interior designed by Mike Rosamilia
The text of this book was set in Adobe Garamond Pro.
Manufactured in the United States of America 0423 OFF
2 4 6 8 10 9 7 5 3 1
Library of Congress Cataloging-in-Publication Data
Names: Burkhart, Jessica, author.
Title: Sweet & bitter rivals / by Jessica Burkhart.
Other titles: Sweet and bitter rivals
Description: First Aladdin hardcover edition. | New York : Aladdin, 2023. |
Series: Saddlehill Academy ; vol 1 | Audience: Ages 9–13. | Audience: Grades 4–6. |
Summary: Seventh grader Abby St. Clair is eager to start another season with her elite riding team at Saddlehill Academy boarding school, competing against her new stepsister—until she starts getting anonymous messages threatening to expose the secret she is desperate to hide.
Identifiers: LCCN 2022053709 (print) | LCCN 2022053710 (ebook) |
ISBN 9781665912884 (pbk) | ISBN 9781665912891 (hc) | ISBN 9781665912907 (ebook)
Subjects: LCSH: Stepsisters—Juvenile fiction. | Sibling rivalry—Juvenile fiction. |
Horse sports—Juvenile fiction. | Boarding schools—Juvenile fiction. | Secrecy—Juvenile fiction. |
CYAC: Stepsisters—Fiction. | Sibling rivalry—Fiction. | Horse sports—Fiction. |
Boarding schools—Fiction. | Schools—Fiction. | Secrets—Fiction.
Classification: LCC PZ7.B92287 Sw 2023 (print) | LCC PZ7.B92287 (ebook) |
DDC 813.6 [Fic]—dc23/eng/20230103
LC record available at https://lccn.loc.gov/2022053709
LC ebook record available at https://lccn.loc.gov/2022053710

To Josh Getzler,
for giving me time and gentle guidance
and helping me pick up all the pieces
needed to build a comeback

Sweet & Bitter Rivals

Welcome Back!

M Y FINGERS SHOOK AS I CLUTCHED the planter balanced in my lap. It was shaped like a hardback book and held a flourishing African violet in a tiny pot in the center. Not just any African violet, of course, but one I'd been raising all summer. They could be *very* temperamental, and I'd managed to keep her alive, so yay! Honestly, the violet was one thing I could count on to provide silent but steady comfort after a summer of turmoil.

Dad eased the car up to the tall iron gates of Saddlehill

Academy, and my breath caught for a second as I tried to take in the majestic campus, from the stone fences to the Gothic architecture to the cobblestoned driveway.

"Look," I said in a whisper to Violet because, of course, that was her name. "Welcome home!"

"What, Abby?" Dad asked from the driver's seat.

My cheeks heated up. "Sorry, Dad. I was talking to Violet."

Dad laughed, but not unkindly. "Don't let me interrupt. I'm glad you're showing your plant-child her new home."

"Well, it would be so rude not to," I said. I touched one of her leaves with my pointer finger. "It's her first day here!"

Yes, I had a plant obsession.

Yes, I talked to them. Sometimes! Okay, a *lot* of the time.

And yes, I'd managed to convince my dad to let me bring seven plants with me to my dorm room at Saddlehill Academy. Seven plants for seventh grade had sounded fair to me!

Saddlehill Academy was a preparatory boarding school nestled just north of Boston. I'd been attending since last year. It had become my home away from home, and I'd spent all of sixth grade learning how to live my best boarding-school-student life.

It had been a bit of a battle to convince my dad to let me

go, but he knew it was my dream to go to boarding school and compete on an equestrian team just like my idol, Sasha Silver. Once I'd pointed out how he wasn't home a lot anyway because of work, he'd finally relented. Plus, it was only about an hour away from my home in Fieldcrest, Massachusetts.

My phone vibrated in the cupholder. I swiped it and saw two new texts from Vivi.

Where are you??

Are you here yet???

Laughing, I typed a quick text back. Pulling in now! ☺

"Let me guess," Dad said, looking at me in the rearview mirror. "Vivi?"

"The one and only," I said, smiling. Vivi had been one of my closest friends at Saddlehill from the moment we'd met last year. We had talked every single day over summer break. She lived in upstate New York, and despite her not living too far away from me, we hadn't been able to make hanging out in person over the summer work. There had been too much going on at home with my dad's wedding to his shiny new wife, Natalie. Sigh.

But this year would make up for it, because Vivi and I had managed to snag a double room in Amherst House—one of the most coveted coed dormitories on campus.

"I'd forgotten how beautiful this place is," Dad said as he eased the car down the long, winding driveway. "Even though I've been here quite a few times."

I nodded. "It feels like forever since I've been here. But also like it was yesterday. So weird."

As excited as I was to see the school, I really couldn't wait to leave and go a few miles down the road to Foxbury Stables, where I kept my horse, Beau, during the school year. He was my *everything*.

As we rolled down the driveway, the beauty of campus wasn't lost on me. Surrounded by woods, Saddlehill's buildings were a rich variety of super-old structures that looked as if they'd come off the pages of a history textbook.

We took a left on Tristan Road, heading toward Amherst. I loved the dormitories at Saddlehill—they weren't typical dorms. They were all actual houses or cottages dotted around campus, and their bedrooms had been converted to dorm rooms.

They had everything from triples to doubles to singles. Each house had a resident advisor who lived in that house too. Second-year students like me were able to apply for a double room. Last year, my only option had been a single, because Saddlehill wanted new students to "focus on adjusting to campus life."

Dad snagged an empty parking spot in front of Amherst House. "Score!" he said. "Let me just check on Natalie and Emery, and then we'll unpack the car."

Oh. Right.

Emery.

For a few minutes, I'd managed to forget all about Emery Flynn. My new stepsister as of this summer. She was a sixth grader who had also been accepted to Saddlehill. Like me, Emery was an equestrian for the Interscholastic Pony League. Unlike me, she was her division's regionals champion and had placed third at nationals. I'd done well during my show season only to choke at regionals and miss going to nationals. So, that made things a *little* awkward between us.

We both rode on the middle school level and had shown in different divisions last year based on our skill level. But Emery had moved up to my division for this year after training with my current instructor, Rebecca, over the summer.

Although riding was an extracurricular at Saddlehill, the school took it seriously. That meant I had access to flexible class schedules that let me do work online or on weekends if necessary so I could ride and train with the equestrian team as much as possible. It was amazing. But what if having to ride with Emery changed everything? I gripped my violet harder and pushed the thought out of my mind.

"Okay, Natalie and Emery will be on campus in a few minutes," Dad said, putting down his phone. "They're going to get Emery moved in, and once you're all set, I'll meet up with them and say goodbye to Emery."

"Oh" was all I said.

"Abby, c'mon," Dad said.

"What?" I asked, trying to keep any hint of attitude out of my tone.

"I know this is all new. It's only been a couple of months since the wedding, so I'm going to give you time to adjust."

I nodded. "Thank you." I blew out an exaggerated breath. "I'm trying, Dad. I promise. I like Natalie and Emery. But I don't know them. At *all*. And we went from strangers to insta-fam this summer, so yeah, I need time."

Before he could say anything back, I flung my door open and hopped out of the car, placing Violet on my seat. I'd come back and get her and my other plant babies in a minute.

I glanced up at Amherst, my new home. According to the

school website, the three-story German stone farmhouse had been built back in the 1700s. It was gable-roofed, with stark white shutters and an attached four-season porch that I could not wait to use. A carriage house, where all ten of the Amherst residents could store boxes and suitcases, sat just in back of the main house.

My eyes roamed over the small courtyard with a couple of stone benches surrounding a tranquil water fountain. The lawn was landscaped to perfection, and there was even an herb garden near the porch. Towering trees flanked the edge of the backyard, and I couldn't wait for the leaves to turn brilliant fall colors soon.

I dug in my pocket for my keys. The front door was open as parents and students carried boxes and luggage inside, but I would need keys for my room if Vivi wasn't there to let me in.

"Why don't you wheel this suitcase up to the house?" Dad suggested. "Leave it beside the porch steps, and I'll carry it up to your room once I get a couple of boxes in there."

"Okay," I said. "Thanks, Dad."

Dad winked at me, then went for the first box in the trunk.

I grabbed the suitcase's handle and tugged it out of the car. Campus was *popping*. It felt as though everyone was moving in at once, even though move-ins had started yesterday. I'd be glad once all the adults left with their cars so campus would go back to the quiet, woodsy space it usually was.

"ABIGAIL ST. CLAIR!"

Laughing, I looked toward the house and smiled at the oh-so-familiar voice. "VIVIENNE MILLS!" I called.

Straining, I pulled my suitcase behind me as I hurried the last few yards to Amherst's porch, where Vivi stood. I let go of the handle and ran up the steps, nearly tackling Vivi in a hug.

"I missed you sooo much!" Vivi said.

We hugged each other hard. "I missed *you* so much!"

After another squeeze, we let go. Vivi was hands down one of the prettiest people I'd ever seen, and today was no exception. Her dark brown skin was flawless, and her curls were pulled back in a high ponytail. She had the softest brown eyes and a smile that lit up her entire face.

"Seeing each other on FaceTime was not enough," Vivi said. "Next summer, you're coming with me to New York City."

"Deal! I can be your assistant and go with you to casting calls."

Vivi grinned. "Exactly!"

Vivi was an actress. She was always at auditions, and

over the summer, she'd even filmed a small role on a big breakout Netflix film! She'd been only a little—okay, a lot—disappointed to find out that her character was attacked and killed by a zombie in the first three seconds of her appearance. But at least she'd had one line—"Ahhh!"

"Hi, Vivi," my dad said, puffing as he came up the stairs carrying one of my boxes.

Vivi gave him a big smile. "Hey, Mr. St. Clair! Oh, our room is on the second floor, and it's the first door on the left."

"C'mon," I said as I motioned to Vivi. "Come with me to the car while I grab some stuff."

I'd been so lucky to meet Vivi last year. We'd become insta-friends from the very first English class we had together. Now that we were back on campus, we'd be spending a ton of time together—no doubt.

"Fair warning," Vivi said. "Our room is a mess right now. I'm pretty much moved in, but my stuff is everywhere until we decorate."

"I can't even believe it!"

"Me either!" Vivi said. "This is going to be the best year ever!"

Vivi reached in and picked up a box from the trunk. "You don't have to do that," I said.

"Pffft," she said. "I'm helping. Deal with it." She tossed me a grin.

She started away from the car as I reached back inside to grab a plant, frowning when I saw that it had turned sideways on the drive.

Vivi turned back to wait for me, but I shook my head. "I'll be right there!"

I took a minute to look it over to make sure my plant was okay and none of the leaves or stems had been damaged. But aside from a tiny bit of spilled gravel, it was fine. Whew.

As I walked up to Amherst, I couldn't keep the bounce out of my step. I was back! And nothing—absolutely nothing— was going to stop me from having the best year ever.

And then . . . I saw her coming out of Amherst House and groaned.

The *one* person who could stop me from having the best year ever.

Selly Hollis.

2

Oh, Greaaat

IF IT'S NOT MY LEAST FAVORITE PERSON
at Saddlehill," Selly called, her eyes narrowing as she
stared me down from her spot near the front door.

I shifted the plant in my arms, and my eyes met Selly's,
but only for a second. I couldn't look her in the eye for long.
Not after . . . *yeah*. She looked perfectly put together—like
always. Her glossy brown hair was styled into easy waves,
and she had a hint of mascara and lip gloss on. It made
me feel like a mess with my barely brushed ponytail and
rumpled T-shirt.

"Good to see you, too," I said. "Although, I'm not gonna lie, I'd hoped we wouldn't run into each other until later. Much later."

"Like when I'm jumping Ember with ease and you're knocking all the rails?"

I sighed. "That's *never* happened, but okay."

We both rode on the same team *and* went to school together. That was more than enough time with Selly!

"Please tell me you're here visiting someone in Amherst," Selly said. "I mean, not that you have any friends. But you're not moving into my house, are you?"

This was going to be *fun*. Not.

I rolled my eyes. "One of my best friends lives here. Oh, and so do I. Get used to it."

"Ooh," Selly said, her brown eyes flashing. "Someone got brave over the summer."

I forced myself to maintain eye contact. "If by brave, you mean not taking your crap? Then yes, I got brave."

Selly grinned, showing white teeth. "We'll see about that."

I had nothing else to say to her. I hurried past her, heading for the door.

"I've heard all about your superstar equestrian little sister,"

Selly said to my back. "It won't be just me that you have to worry about this year."

I tilted my chin up and kept walking, trying to project an air of confidence. But my stomach flipped. If only Selly knew what I'd done. But I'd have to do everything to prevent that from happening.

A couple of hours later, I hugged Dad on the Amherst lawn. We'd moved every box inside, and he'd helped me unload them and carry the empty boxes to the carriage house. He'd raised an eyebrow at the collection of sneakers I'd brought with me, but I'd started running over the summer and, hello, I needed as many comfy shoe options as possible.

For a second, I closed my eyes, thinking about what it would be like if Mom were here. If she'd stayed and not abandoned us when I was seven. But I didn't want to think about her. Not today and certainly not now. If I did, the familiar wave of sadness tinged with anger would overshadow everything about this day.

"Abs?" Dad's question almost made me jump.

"Sorry," I said. "I was just . . . thinking about Mom."

"I am too," Dad said. "I wish she were here to see you move

in today." Dad was always so diplomatic about Mom. "But it's going to be okay. I may not be"—he gestured around—"right here. But I will always be here for you. No matter what. I hope, with time, you come to lean on Natalie, too. She cares about you, Abby."

I started to protest, but he raised a hand. "Natalie is not going to replace your mom, I promise. I hope that eventually we'll be a family. You, me, Natalie, and Emery. But it's not going to happen overnight, and that's okay."

I swallowed back tears. "I don't need a mom," I whispered.

I had Dad, and he was all I needed, even if my feelings about my mom went from hating her to missing her. Wherever she was.

Dad had spent a lot of time with a lawyer who had tried to track her down to serve her with divorce papers, but no one could find her. The divorce had finally been granted by the court, but what if she didn't know? Even after everything she'd done, what if this—us trying to move on—hurt her? But maybe she deserved it? I wasn't sure.

Like mine, Dad's moods about her changed often too. Over the years, he'd gone from furious that she'd left me home alone to missing her and wanting her back to trying to forget about her.

Dad touched my cheek with one hand. "Sweetheart, it's time for us to figure out our lives without her, okay?"

I took a shaky breath. Even though I'd known it was the truth for a long, long time, it still didn't get any easier to hear. Even if I wasn't sure I ever wanted to see her again.

"Together?" I asked.

"Together," Dad said, holding eye contact with me. He pushed his round glasses up on his nose in one of his most familiar gestures.

I brushed loose strands of hair off my face and took a few more breaths. "Okay," I said. "Thank you for everything, Dad." I stepped closer to him, squeezing him one last time.

"Of course," he said. "You needed more muscle to help you get all those boxes of shoes inside. I had to help."

I gasped in mock outrage. Holding up my right arm, I flexed. The tiniest muscle ever popped out. "Wait till you see me next. I'm going to hit the gym every day! You won't even recognize me."

We laughed, and Dad touched my cheek. "This is going to be a great year for you, Abby. I'm so proud of you, and I can't wait to watch you accomplish so many wonderful things. And yes, that will include all this gym time you're about to experience. I'm sure you'll get *very* ripped."

"Thanks, Dad. I love you."

"I love you more," he said. "Gonna go check on Beau?"

I nodded. "Definitely. After I change, I'll grab a bus to the stable and see how he's doing."

"Keep an eye on Emery, too, Abs. You sure you don't want to come with me to her dorm?"

I'd already declined twice. I shook my head. "No, I want to see Beau."

With that, I waved goodbye to Dad, and he slowly pulled away from the curb, heading to Emery's dorm.

Something twinged in my chest. *There's nothing to get upset about,* I told myself. Dad had made sure I was completely settled in, and of course he would go check on Emery. Heck, he'd even invited me! But I didn't want to see Emery with her mom today. Not when mine wouldn't even tell me where she was.

It felt weird to have Dad here and not hanging with me, even though he'd just left my dorm. I knew he was trying his best to bring our blended family together, but he was so clueless about what I really felt. It was kind of my fault, I guess. We'd both been so broken after Mom left that it had taken him a long, long time to smile again. I'd made it my mission not to say or do anything to make him that sad ever again. So I tried to pretend I was happy and okay even if I wasn't.

Sigh. This would get easier, right? I tried to stuff my feelings down and not obsess over it. There was too much to do this weekend.

I sent a quick text to Thea Song, my other best friend on campus. I'm at school! Gonna change and go groom Beau before the meeting! Unlike Vivi, Thea was a rider, and I had a feeling she'd want to check on Chaos Gremlin, her horse.

I turned back to Amherst House and headed inside. In the kitchen, I poured myself a glass of pink lemonade and checked my email on my phone.

From: Dean Paulson
To: Abigail St. Clair
August 26 at 10:45 a.m.
Subject: A request

Dear Ms. St. Clair,
Welcome back for another year! As I'm sure
you're aware, you will need service hours
this year to pass seventh grade. I'd like you

to begin those hours by giving Emery Flynn a peer-led tour of campus. Also, please bring her to Assembly.

Don't forget to log these hours for the year. Please let me know when you receive this message.

All best,

Dean Paulson

It took me only a few seconds to write him back.

From: Abigail St. Clair

To: Dean Paulson

August 26 at 10:49 a.m.

Subject: Re: A request

Hello, Dean Paulson,

I got your message. I'd be happy to give Emery a tour of campus. Thank you for thinking of me and my service hours.

All best,

Abigail St. Clair

After I got upstairs, I texted Emery.

Hey! Hope you're settling in okay. 😊 I got a message from the dean, and he wants me to give you a tour of campus. Wanna do that tomorrow? Lmk!

"Sheesh, Abby," I muttered to myself. "Stop rambling."

But things were still awkward between us. Emery had always been perfectly polite to me, but we were basically strangers. Well, strangers who shared a house since my dad and I had moved in with Emery and Natalie this summer. The most we'd shared before that was a stable that was big enough that we'd never ridden together or even talked before our parents had started dating.

And I'd gone from having a single parent to having two adults around. Seeing Emery and her mom together had gotten a bit easier, but I still couldn't help but look at them and wish my own mom had cared enough about me to stick around.

But as I walked into my room, where Vivi was busy decorating, what I saw made me smile, and it helped whoosh away the bad feelings.

While I'd been saying bye to Dad, Vivi had spread a shaggy yellow rug—one I'd put on our shared room-decor Pinterest board—in the center of the gleaming hardwood floor. I kicked off my flip-flops and walked onto it.

"Ooh, this is so soft," I said.

"Isn't it?" Vivi asked. "I love it."

I walked over to the full-length mirror that was set up in a corner of the room and caught a glimpse of my reflection. Strands of my long brown hair had escaped my ponytail, and I brushed them away from my eyes. My blue-green eyes matched the T-shirt I had on, and I made a mental note to wash it soon so I could wear it again. It made my eyes pop.

The room looked so cute already! Our twin beds were nestled by a large window on one end of the room. At the other end, near the door, we had small desks near our closets. And we'd scored a nonworking brick fireplace with a cute white mantel. Vivi had already put a couple of yummy-scented candles on it.

My phone buzzed in my hand.

Emery: Hi! I'm free tomorrow whenever you are. I'm already over unpacking, and it will be good for me to see the campus, I think. Lmk when you're on your way. 😊

I plopped onto my bare mattress. "Argh," I said. "The dean is making me give Emery a tour of campus, so I asked if she wanted to do it tomorrow. Today's kinda busy."

"It really is," Vivi said. "I have to go to the admin office and turn in some forms in a few minutes. Then run to the campus bookstore."

"And I'm going to groom Beau, and there's an unmounted meeting at the stable—a quick welcome-back thing."

Vivi nodded. "Cool. I'll have to come by and see Beau soon!"

That made me smile. Vivi was not a horse girl, but she would listen to me talk about horses for hours and even ask questions and remember stuff. If it was important to me, it was important to her.

"You definitely have to," I said. "He'll help me shake off my meh mood."

"Why 'meh'?"

I sat up and shrugged. "It's dumb."

"Doubt it."

"No, it is," I said. "I'm being a brat." I sighed. "I'm annoyed at Emery. I know it's not her fault, but my dad went to her dorm after he moved me in."

"I'm failing to see where you were a brat," Vivi said. She lowered herself onto the chaise lounge near the fireplace.

"I'm in a bad mood because my dad went to see Emery. After he finished spending hours moving me in. I have zero reason to be upset about him going to see his"—I paused—"*other* daughter."

"I mean, how could that not be weird?" Vivi asked. "This has all happened so fast. You go to one horse show and boom—your dad meets her mom, and next thing you know, they're dating."

"And I didn't even know Emery from before," I said, a whine creeping into my tone. "Sure, I'd seen her around at shows. I kind of knew who she was. But we'd never talked! And once our parents started dating, we still stayed away from each other until they forced us to hang out at dinners to 'get to know' each other."

"And now you're all moved into her house. Barely. You just got everything unpacked, and it was time to come here. Oh, and surprise! She wants to come too. So, yeah, you're definitely allowed to feel weird. I would."

I smiled at her. "Thank you. For all of that."

"You don't need to thank me," she said. "Go see your horse, I'll run my errands, and then we can decorate our room, okay?"

"I'm so in."

That talk with Vivi made me feel lighter than I had all day. She was good like that. And as I headed to grab a bus to the stable, I shook off my meh mood with thoughts of seeing my guy, my boy, my boo—Beau.

Reunited, and It Feels So Good

As I WALKED TOWARD THE STABLE, MY phone buzzed with a text.

Thea: Already here with Chaos! Come find us outside! 😀

I almost danced as I walked toward the stable, overwhelmed by the beauty and the excitement over seeing Thea. Even though I'd been here countless times, it never stopped being any less impressive. I'd missed it over the summer when I'd been riding at my home barn in Fieldcrest.

The stable was two stories. The lower level housed horses

and was where we spent most of our time, and a smaller second floor had the trainer and instructor offices and a common area for meetings. My favorite parts were the sweeping arches that made up the building's front exterior and the iron spires on the roof that made the stable look almost like a medieval castle. Plenty of windows let in lots of light, and I loved their dark brown shutters.

The front lawn was lush with shrubs, leafy hedges, and red maple trees. The building backed up to woods and a river, which made the exquisite stable look even more magnificent. Thankfully, things were fairly quiet right now before everyone arrived for the meeting. I stepped inside, letting my eyes adjust. I couldn't help but smile as I looked around.

"It's so good to be back," I said in a whisper to myself.

Every inch of wood gleamed, from the ceiling to the stall walls to the stall doors. The lower halves of the stalls were all stone and painted a stark, sharp white. Iron pendant lights gave off a warm glow and made the stable aisle feel cozy despite it being huge.

I walked down the aisle, looking for Beau. When I spotted his elegant head sticking out over a stall door toward the end of the aisle, it took everything in me not to break into a run toward my bay gelding.

"Hiii, boy!" I said when I got to him. I reached up, rubbing his forehead and smoothing his black forelock over part of his blaze. "I missed you so much." I'd been so busy packing and getting ready for school that it had been a few days since I'd seen Beau. I always got nervous about my precious cargo being on the road, no matter how many times we'd traveled for shows or clinics.

During the summer, I boarded Beau at Bayview—my old stable at home. I'd spent nearly every day at Bayview over the summer to ride and care for Beau. It wasn't unusual for me to go a day or two here and there without seeing him, but I always missed him. I'd grown up as an only child, and Beau was the closest thing I'd had to a sibling. Even if he was furry.

Now this stable was going to be mine and Emery's. We both competed in Area 1, which covered our state of Massachusetts and the rest of New England. Last year was my first time riding for Foxbury's team. Emery had competed for Bayview. Foxbury was one of the top competitive barns in our area and almost always made it from regionals to area finals to nationals.

And this year, just like the last, we'd be up against Sasha's old stable—Canterwood Crest. But they weren't taking home all the blue ribbons this year. Some of those were mine, and I was ready to fight for them.

I let myself into the stall, my boots sinking into the deep, clean sawdust. "You were a good boy, huh?" I asked him.

Beau slowly blinked at me, lowering his head so he could put his muzzle in my hands. I kissed his head and looked over every inch of him, even though I knew he'd been looked after during the hour-long trailer ride from Fieldcrest. Still, I didn't fully exhale until I saw for myself that he was in perfect condition.

Beau was a Dutch Warmblood and an average 16.1 hands high, so he wasn't particularly tall for his breed. That helped me, since I wasn't tall either. "We're going to go see Chaos and Thea," I told him. "So, let's get out of your stall and go find them."

With Beau beside me and his grooming bag slung over my shoulder, I headed back down the stable aisle. I resisted the urge to pet the velvety muzzles sticking out of stall doors. Some horses nickered at me as I passed, and happiness swirled in my belly. Nothing—absolutely nothing—made me happier than horses.

There was zero about them that I disliked. Okay, mucking

stalls I could do without. But everything else was part of the way I showed Beau how much I loved and cared about him. Any amount of time I got to spend with him made us that much closer and more bonded, and to succeed in the show ring, I wanted and needed Beau to be my partner in every way possible. Plus, he deserved to feel appreciated. Grooming and caring for him was how I showed my appreciation.

I needed him in the best possible headspace going into the show season. We were going to prove just how much we belonged on Foxbury's IPL team. I hoped the Canterwood riders were ready to be dethroned, because this year? It was *on*.

Tell Me Everything

OUTSIDE THE STABLE, I SQUEALED WHEN I saw a very familiar black-haired girl and her bright chestnut gelding.

"Thea!" I said.

"Abbyyy!"

I hurried over to my other best friend, and we threw our free arms around each other.

"I missed you!" I said. "It's so good to see you!"

She grinned, tossing her ponytail. Thea was easily three inches taller than me, so I felt like a shrimp next to her.

"You too! I love summer, but argh, I missed seeing you every day."

I let Beau stretch his neck to sniff muzzles with Chaos so the two could say hello.

"The boys missed each other too," I said. "They're so cute together."

"They really are. Want to go groom them by the big outdoor arena? The one with the shade? We can watch people practice from there."

"Yes, please," I said. We had an hour until our welcome-back meeting with our instructor, Rebecca.

Quickly, I reached over and patted Chaos's neck. We walked our horses side by side to the tie rings near the arena, settling them under two leafy oak trees so we'd have some shade on this hot day.

"So, tell me everything," Thea said. "I mean, I know we texted all summer except for when I was visiting my grandparents in Korea, but still. We're face-to-face now!"

I put down my grooming kit and dug around for Beau's hoof pick. "I'm so glad to be back. It was a weird summer—moving out of my house and into the Flynns'. I didn't even get to unpack all my stuff before school started, so I don't know when it will start to feel like home. Maybe never?"

"I hope not," Thea said. "I know how hard moving was on you. I'm glad it's over, but I wish you'd felt at home."

I shrugged one shoulder. "At least I'm here now, and I can focus all my energy on riding and school."

"And hanging out with meee!"

"Obviously!"

Thea reached for a dandy brush. "Have you seen Emery since you got to school?"

"Nope. But I came straight here after my dad got me moved in. I'm sure she'll be here for the meeting, though."

Thea nodded. "Is your dad still all, 'Be Emery's best friend, Abby'?"

"All. The. Time. I know he wants us to be these super-close sisters. But I need time. I'm sure she does too."

"Absolutely." Thea looked over at me, raising an eyebrow. "And did you tell your dad you need time? Or keep everything in and pretend it's fine like always?"

"I told him! Kind of on the car ride over, but I told him."

"Well, good. That's a start."

"Honestly, it feels like a relief to get out of their house and come here," I said, shaking my head a bit. "I still look at Natalie and think about my mom."

Thea peered around Chaos's shoulder and shot me a sympathetic smile. "I bet."

I'd look at Natalie doing everyday, regular mom things, and I'd flash back to the last time I'd seen mine. How one evening when my dad had been at work, she'd walked down the driveway and hopped into an Uber—leaving seven-year-old me all alone and waiting by the window. My dad had come home an hour or two later and found me still watching and waiting for her. She never came back.

My dad had done his absolute best to step up and take care of me, but he'd been gone a lot with his medical tech company, so I'd spent a lot of time with my aunt, who had basically moved in to stay with me. It had almost seemed as if Dad thought he could work away his sadness and anger. I'd been so terrified of losing him, too, that I'd tried to be the perfect daughter. It was a lot of pressure, but slowly, it had become something I was used to.

But keeping things from my dad had bled over into other areas of my life too, especially with my friends. It had taken almost all of last year before I'd finally started telling Thea and Vivi when something was wrong in my life. But they'd shown me that they weren't going to ditch me, and it was a good thing to open up to them.

"Maybe the move will feel better eventually," Thea said slowly. "It could have just made things even harder on you to stay in your childhood home, surrounded by all your mom's stuff."

I chewed on the inside of my cheek. "I'm not sure if it was good or not yet," I said. "But my dad seems happier, so maybe it was the right thing to do."

Time would tell. For now, I was away at school and wouldn't have to deal with the uncomfortableness of living in someone else's house. My dad had tried to make the move as easy on me as possible, but it still had been a turbulent time. I'd gone back and forth from crying one minute over losing my family home to standing on the lawn of Natalie and Emery's house with my chin jutted out, glad I'd been given the chance to get away from all the memories in my old house. All the memories with Mom.

Thea stepped around Chaos, making eye contact with me. "You have to be happy too, Abs. Not just your dad. But no matter what, don't forget that I've got you."

"Thank you. I know you do." I smiled. "But enough about me! How are you? How was moving in? Tell me *all* the things!"

Thea flicked a body brush over Chaos's back and haunches.

"Moving in was pretty easy, which is good because I'm also going to be busy helping Cora get settled on campus. She's so much braver than I was at her age, though. She's not nervous at all about being here."

"Ah, to be a bold, young sixth grader," I said.

Cora was Thea's little sister, and they were super close after surviving a serious car crash a couple of years ago. Thea had walked away relatively unhurt, but Cora had lost her left leg below the knee.

"Right? She's been at Saddlehill for a few hours, and she's so chill already."

For a second, I felt a rush of jealousy at their relationship. "Is she excited to ride a new horse?" I asked.

Like us, Cora was on the IPL. She'd been an equestrian before the accident, and Thea had told me how she'd refused to give up riding even after the crash.

"She's thrilled. I can't wait to see what lesson horse she gets."

"It doesn't sound like she needs any encouragement or advice," I said, "but if she does and you're busy or something, send her my way."

"I will. Thanks, Abs."

We fell into an easy chatter as we groomed our horses

and watched a few students practice in the arena, which made me want to ride. But there was no time today. Soon, though, I would be back in the saddle. I couldn't wait to kick off this year and, hopefully, show off the improvements I'd made over the summer break.

We finished grooming the horses a few minutes before the meeting and led them back to their stalls. Inside Beau's stall, I unclipped his lead line and let him free. I checked his hay net and water bucket, fishing a couple of stray pieces of hay out of the water.

My mind wandered to Thea and Cora, and I thought about how the concept of a sister was still so foreign to me. Sure, Emery and I had only been stepsisters for six weeks, and I knew it would take time to feel a bond. But maybe one day, I'd have a relationship with Emery like Thea had with Cora.

I hugged Beau tight and took a deep breath, squeezing his neck. "Things are changing, boy. Emery's here. Here as in this stable and Saddlehill. It's weird." Draping an arm over Beau's neck, I ran my fingers through his mane. "I know I've done nothing but complain to you about Emery and the whole move and her coming to Saddlehill, but she's actually not awful," I said. "She's not a spoiled kid with an evil stepmother who hates me and is out to steal my dad." I shrugged. "She's been nice to me so far, and even when I worry that she's a better rider than I am, it just means I need to work that much harder on my own skills."

And I would. There was nothing that was going to stand in my way this year of becoming the top rider on our circuit. The champion. The one going to nationals. The one *winning* nationals.

"Honestly," I said to Beau, "there's already plenty for me to worry about."

Immediately, my mind went to one of my biggest worries: Selly and what I'd done. Even though it had been an accident, it made my stomach churn when I thought about it. But I couldn't fix it or take it back. Now, the only thing I could do was ensure that she never found out.

I hugged Beau again, dropping a kiss on his muzzle. "I'll see you tomorrow, boy. I've got to run to a meeting."

With a final glance at Beau, I left him munching hay in his stall and headed to meet Rebecca and the rest of the team. In this moment, I felt more ready than ever to make it all the way to the top this show season. Beau was ready, and so was I.

5

Sasha + Heather = Dream Team

I REACHED THE NEAREST OUTDOOR ARENA and found it filling with riders, but I made sure to steer clear of Selly and her BFF Nina once I heard Selly's loud laughter from the other end of the arena. Thankfully, there were so many people there that I doubted they'd even notice me for a while. I spotted a familiar girl with ash-blond hair. "Maia!" I said.

"Abby!" Maia, a super-friendly freshman from Saddlehill, hurried over and threw an arm around me.

"How are you?" I asked. "How's life?"

"Good!" the older girl said. "I spent two weeks at riding camp at—"

"*Canterwood,*" I said at the exact same time she did. I'd seen plenty of pics on her stories.

Maia laughed. "I still can't believe that happened. I actually took lessons at Canterwood Crest Academy."

I groaned. "Ugh. You got to learn from Sasha. The Sasha Silver. Like . . . oh my god!"

"Right? The legend herself. Heather Fox was there at the end too. The dream duo."

"Both of them?" I tried not to shriek.

"*Both.* It was really surprising after all the rumors of drama and rivalry between them. They were very friendly with each other." Maia waggled her eyebrows.

"*Stop,*" I said. "That's wild. I'm going to combust from jealousy even though I'm really, really happy for you."

"Well, rumor has it that Sasha and Heather are teaching an exclusive winter clinic, so . . ."

I had to cover my mouth to keep from squealing. "Really? Omigod, I follow Sasha on social media, but I didn't see that news! I'm *so* trying to get in!"

"Hey, hey!" A friendly voice made Maia and me look behind us.

"Keir!" I said, hugging him.

He hugged Maia next, and I couldn't help but smile. Keir was another member of my riding team. Like me, he was in seventh grade at Saddlehill. He was one of the nicest and cutest guys I'd ever met, with the biggest smile, light brown skin, and cropped black hair.

"It's been way too long since I've seen you," Keir said.

"I know," Maia said, "but here we are—all ready to kick butt this year!"

She waved Thea over, and we all chatted away and said our hellos after a summer apart.

The team was big—we had students in grades five through twelve from various area schools—but Rebecca kept our practices smaller in size based on our experience level, and sometimes mixed older, more experienced riders into my lessons. So I'd done some practicing with Maia and the other older riders. My group would look different this year with Emery as an addition. Speaking of which, I hadn't seen her. I broke away from my friends and went looking for my stepsister.

It took me a few minutes of weaving through the crowd before I spotted her. She stood off to the side of the arena, arms wrapped across her chest. She stared at her phone, then glanced up, her hazel eyes darting around as she played with the end of her honey-blond ponytail. My heart twinged a bit. I knew what she was doing—trying to look busy so she didn't appear so alone.

"Hey," I called as I walked over to her.

She smiled, relief lighting up her face. "Hi!"

Even if things were weird between us, I wasn't going to leave her standing there alone.

"Come with me," I said. "I've got two people I want you to meet."

She thumbed the PopSocket on her phone. "I'm sure you're busy. I'm okay!"

"I'm not. C'mon." I motioned for her to follow me, nodding toward two younger girls talking to each other. "That's Wren and Zoe," I said. "They're both sixth graders who go to Saddlehill too. I haven't talked to them a ton, but when I have, they've been really sweet."

Emery turned her phone over and over in her hand, her eyes wide. "Wren and Zoe," she repeated. "Okay."

We walked up to Wren and Zoe, and the two girls greeted us with smiles.

"Hey," I said. "Fancy meeting you both here!"

Zoe laughed, flashing a mouthful of braces. "Right?"

"Who'd have thunk it?" Wren asked. She tucked a lock of chin-length red hair behind her ear.

"I don't want to interrupt you two, but I did want to say hi and introduce you to someone. This is my . . ." I paused, the word "stepsister" heavy and unfamiliar in my mouth. "This is Emery Flynn. It's her first year at Saddlehill, and she was just accepted to our riding team."

The younger girls smiled, unaware that I was yelling at myself for not introducing Emery the way I should have. Was it that hard to say one little word?

"Hi," Emery said shyly. "Nice to meet you."

"Welcome to the riding team!" Zoe said. "And to Saddlehill. What house are you in?"

And just like that, the three younger girls fell into easy chatter. I headed back over to Thea and the rest of my friends as Rebecca walked into the arena with a giant smile on her face.

"Hello, riders!" she said. "Welcome back to Foxbury! Or, for those who are new, just plain old welcome!"

Cheers and applause rang out. Rebecca was like a family member to me. An aunt, of sorts, who kicked my butt when it was time to get in gear, held my hand when I needed comfort, and pushed me to my limits in my sport. There had been times last year when I'd been sure I couldn't spend another moment in the saddle without screaming. But Rebecca hadn't let me give up. She knew exactly how hard to push and when to back off. She was the best riding instructor I could ever imagine having.

"This enthusiasm is wonderful," she said. "For those of you who have been away over the summer, it's so great to see you and have our team back together. I missed seeing everyone." She raised an eyebrow. "I'm curious to see what you've learned if you've been away from my clutches. And, I admit, I'm also excited to see what bad habits you've picked up that I need to train out of you with no stirrups for a week."

We all laughed. "No Stirrups November" was Rebecca's favorite time of the year. It was more important to her than *any* holiday. Even Christmas!

"Now," she said, "we'll have more time to chat and discuss all my expectations and such this week when we meet again, but today I want you to think about and remember a few things. First, always remember that you are part of a team. You always have a network of support from the other riders in this community. You may feel alone in the ring or on a course, but I've always got your back. And your other teammates should too."

We applauded.

"This year is going to be a great one, I can feel it," Rebecca said. "Whatever you put into riding, into this team, you will get back. I expect you to put one hundred percent of yourself into riding, whether we're in a lesson or at a show. Laziness is not tolerated. I demand that you work as hard as your fellow riders who are giving it their all." She took a deep breath. "If you're not willing to go above and beyond what I ask, our competition teams are not for you."

I nodded. Still, what she said made me anxious. This team, this sport was intimidating. Rebecca was intimidating! As kind as she was, she also made zero apologies for being demanding. It made me a better equestrian, hands down, but it was also a lot of pressure.

"I expect you to care for your horses," Rebecca said. "We have grooms who help, yes, but I need to see you pitching in too. The riders on my team love these animals as much as I do. Horses do so much for us, and the least we can do is give them proper care. If you can't be bothered to care for your own horse, or the one assigned to you, then you are not a good fit for my team."

I didn't have to worry about that. I was head over heels for Beau and completely dedicated to caring for him. It made me feel good to make him happy.

"Equine education is a critical component of my team as well," Rebecca said. "There will be quizzes, tests, and oral and written exams. If learning about horses and their care doesn't interest you, again, there are other instructors here who offer more relaxed riding lessons and noncompetitive riding. If that would fit you better, please let me know."

No way. I grinned, shaking my head. This was what I wanted. This was what we *all* wanted. All of us gathered here as part of Foxbury's Interscholastic Pony League.

"All right, all right," Rebecca said. "I know you've all got a million things to do this weekend, so I'll dismiss our meeting. But don't ever forget that you're part of a team. Win or lose. I'm extremely proud, humbled, and thrilled to work with each one of you this year. Are you all ready to work?"

"Yeaaah!" I cheered as everyone around me burst into whistles and applause.

"That's what I like to hear!" Rebecca said. "See you in the arena!"

And with that, cheers broke out again. I clapped until my

hands stung and the cheers of my teammates rang in my ears. I looked over, spotting Emery. The nervous look on her face was gone. She smiled, cheering and clapping along with everyone. She was going to be okay. That much was clear.

As for me? This was exactly where I belonged, and I wanted to win this year. More than ever before. Whatever it took.

That Was a Choice

"**D**O WE WANT PIZZA, PIZZA, OR PIZZA?"
Vivi asked.

I tapped my chin, pretending to think. "I'm torn. Pizza sounds so good. But so does pizza. I guess we should get pizza?"

"Good call," Vivi said. "It was a tough decision. But let's order pizza."

Vivi ordered a half-cheese, half-pepperoni from the local pizza place that was one of many restaurants included in our meal plan and allowed to deliver on campus.

While we waited for our food, we unpacked and chatted. I went over to the open boxes of plants I'd brought, picking them up one by one. My little green babies.

"Ooh, that planter is cute," Vivi said. "It's a gyroid, right?"

"Yup! I'm slowly building a collection of planters from my fave games."

I had a Bulbasaur planter too, and this gyroid was my first, from *Animal Crossing*. It held a cute angel wings plant, aka a bunny ears cactus. The thick pads on the plant were covered in fuzz that looked like fur, and they grew in ear-shaped pairs.

"Making a mental note of that for your Christmas gifts," Vivi said. She picked up one of the succulents, which had green leaves tinged with red, and stared at it. "This one's pretty. What is it?"

"That's a Campfire *Crassula*," I said. "It's known to grow really fast, and it'll get these pretty little white flowers next spring."

"Aw, cute. And this one?"

I smiled at my Mario warp pipe planter. "That's a jade plant. A *Crassula ovata*. It's a lucky plant."

Vivi gently touched its small, treelike shape. "Lucky plant, huh?"

I nodded. "Yup. It's going to get a lot bigger too."

That made her eyes widen a bit. "Just how much bigger?"

"Wellll, it'll take time, of course, but they can grow up to six feet tall."

"Abby!"

"It won't be this year!" I promised. I pointed to an empty corner in our room. "But in case it gets a ridiculous growth spurt—and it won't—it can go right over there."

Vivi hung her head for a second, shaking it. "That plant's already giving you luck, because I'm not making you find it a different home."

I laughed. "Noted. I'm so glad the luck is working." I nodded toward the other two succulents—a Black Prince and a jelly bean sedum. "Those will stay small. So, whew."

"Whew, indeed," Vivi said. "For you." But she winked at me to let me know she wasn't seriously mad or anything, then went over to keep organizing her space. She'd strung fairy lights over the wall above her desk, and they gave Vivi's work space a cozy vibe.

I smiled, looking at all my unboxed plants. Taking care of the family houseplants had fallen to me when Mom left. They'd started to wilt and shrivel, and I'd refused to let them die. So I'd figured out how to care for them, and soon I'd become the green thumb in the family, and everyone came to me with plant questions.

I dug into the small box beside my bed that I'd left sealed until now. It held a few of my most precious possessions, one of which was a silver picture frame with a photo of Mom and me that had been on my nightstand ever since I could remember.

Running my thumb over the glass, I stared at the picture. Mom's warm hazel eyes were focused on the camera. Or, rather, on the person taking the photo—Dad. She was crouched down next to five-year-old me, and I held a single daisy out to her for the taking. I looked at Mom as if she was my whole world. She kind of had been. Now I had moments where I felt nothing but fury when I looked at her photo and other days when it made me sad. And, on rare occasions, I could look at the photo and feel happy when I thought about that time, because it *had* been a good moment.

Vivi came over and nodded at the photo. "You brought it," she said softly.

"I wish I could have left it at ho—" I swallowed. "I mean, at the Flynns'. I tried! But I decided I had to bring it after I'd already put tape on the box, so I had to open it again and stick the frame inside."

"You don't have much left of your mom," Vivi said. "So I think it's good that you brought it if it's something you're okay with having around."

I nodded, my eyes glued to the photo. Part of me wished I could have left the photo at home. But the other part of me didn't want to ever be without it. It was true: I didn't have much left of Mom—especially post-move—and that photo was one of the few things I'd kept. Together, Dad and I had donated most of Mom's things to charity, and it had made me feel good to envision other people being helped by her belongings.

"It makes me happy and sad to look at this picture," I said. "I think about how close we all were back then, and how things are now. It makes me worry about how they'll be in the future, too."

Vivi frowned. "What? Why?"

"My dad's already busy. All the time. He's always working from his laptop or phone or tablet. Always!" I hesitated. "Which is fine. Most of the time. I'm used to it. But now with Emery and Natalie . . ."

"You're worried he won't have any time for you," Vivi said.

"Exactly."

Dad didn't have time for me before Emery. There was no way he'd have time for me now.

"Well, I do know he loves you a lot," Vivi said. "And maybe there will be a kind of adjustment period while he figures everything out. But if he doesn't make time for you, all you have to do is tell me."

I tilted my head. "Oh?"

She nodded. "Yup. I'll call him so fast on your behalf and demand he pay attention to my bestie."

That made me smile. Vivi would do it too. As uncomfortable as I was with the Flynns, I also didn't want to ruin this for my dad. He'd spent a lot of time in therapy after Mom had left, healing. He deserved to be happy, and he needed dependable, steady Abby, who was just fine on her own.

"You're the best," I said. "Thanks."

"I gotchu, Abby. I think everything will work out. Give it some time."

We hugged, then went back to unpacking, talking about Vivi and how her summer had been, with all the countless auditions she'd done.

"Pizza's here," Vivi said a few minutes later. "Want to go eat downstairs?"

"Sure!" Nothing better to combat anxiety than pizza with Vivi.

We headed downstairs, and while Vivi met the delivery person, I grabbed plates and napkins. We went into the common room, which was a living room with a giant TV, a fireplace, and massive built-in bookshelves. No one else was in here, which suited me just fine. We ate pizza and flicked on an old episode of one of our mutual fave TV shows about paranormal investigations.

"C'mon in here," someone said, their voice carrying from just outside the room.

"Nooo," I said under my breath. I'd already had one run-in with Selly today.

But she walked right into the living room with her best friend—Nina Wilkerson—in tow.

"Aw, boo, the losers are here," Selly said once she spotted Vivi and me.

"Nice to see you, too, Selly," Vivi said. "I missed your jokes all summer."

"Did you move in here too?" I asked Nina, barely holding back a groan.

"No, I'm in Charles House. I'm just here to hang out with Selly," she said, running a hand through her cropped light brown hair.

Charles House was where Emery lived too.

"I have a single anyway," Selly said. "Like I'd want to share a room with someone."

Sheesh. Rude to Nina much?

Vivi quietly snorted. "I don't know about everyone else, but I'm guessing no one wanted to share with you, either. Especially after the way you treat your friends."

Nina pressed her lips together, not saying anything. I didn't get it. Why was she friends with Selly? Nina had been nice to me once upon a time. Now she was being brainwashed by the meanest girl in school and acting like a friendship with Selly was worth taking her being a horrible friend.

"Oh, please," Selly said, rolling her eyes. "You wish. I could fill this entire house with my friends. Easy."

"I doubt that," I said. "But whatever." I turned to look at Vivi. "I'm finished eating. You?"

She nodded. "Want to keep unpacking?"

"Most definitely." I picked up the TV remote and lightly tossed it to Selly. "Enjoy!"

I gathered up my plate, cup, and napkins while Selly navigated over to YouTube.

"We're going to watch last year's Fieldcrest Classic," Selly said. "Are you sure you don't want to stay?"

My body flashed cold and then hot. I gritted my teeth, trying to force a neutral expression on my face. I didn't want Selly to know that what she'd said had bugged me.

"We're good, thanks," I said.

The only reason she'd said that was to get under my skin. Last year I'd shown in the Fieldcrest Classic and had made mistake after mistake. I'd forgotten parts of my dressage test, had knocked four rails in jumping, and had fallen on cross-country *after* Beau already refused a jump and almost dumped me over the rail and into the water on the other side. It had been the worst performance of my career, and it still rattled me to think about it.

There were a zillion and one horse shows to watch on YouTube—it was something Thea and I did all the time—but there was zero reason for Selly and Nina to watch *that* show.

"You sure?" Nina asked, smirking. "You might learn something from all your many, *many* past mistakes!"

Selly laughed. "And when we're done, we're watching

that recorded livestream of Jasmine King's show from a few weeks ago."

Even the mention of the older Olympic-hopeful rider made me frown.

"Why?" I asked. "Jasmine is Sasha's archrival."

"Exactly." Selly grinned. "She's my favorite."

"She's . . . Jas is reckless! She pushes her horse way too much, and she has the *worst* reputation. She's mean to everyone!"

"Nah, Jas is so cool," Nina said. "Did you see her at the South Carolina event over the summer? She was flawless. As if Sasha could ever."

I shook my head. "Jasmine King is so awful, she was expelled from Canterwood! Everyone knows it! She's a legend in all the worst ways! How is that cool?"

"As I said, my fave," Selly said.

Clenching my teeth, I left the living room without a word, trying not to look as if I was in a hurry. But I wasn't going to spend another second near those two—not until we were in the arena.

Sweets, Treats, and Gimme Those Deets

LATE THE FOLLOWING MORNING, I MET Emery so I could give her a tour. I was in such a good mood from last night—it had been the perfect welcome-back evening with Vivi. We'd made a list of scary movies that had come out over the summer to save and watch together.

We'd watched *Up All Nite* on my laptop, and we did stay up way too late before falling asleep, talking about our mutual love of horror films.

"Okay, so before we begin your official tour, let's get

something at Sweets N' Treats," I said. "And, of course, it's on me as your tour guide."

"Thanks!"

"Sweets is just one of the handful of cafés and restaurants on campus," I said. "We have lots here. And if you want to order out, there's a list of approved places that are allowed to deliver on campus."

"Cool," Emery said. "I love trying new places to eat."

We turned onto the sidewalk to Sweets. The space was one of my faves on campus. It was a Victorian cottage complete with a black wrought-iron railing and a tiny gated entrance. Emery held open the door for me, and we stepped inside.

"Wow, this place is cute!" Emery said. "It feels so cozy."

The small room had yellow accents on the walls and several menu boards written in beautiful calligraphy. Antique chairs were tucked under tiny tables, and each table had a vase of cheery sunflowers.

"It does have maximum cozy cottage vibes," I said. "But, like, Candy Land coziness because of all the colors and the candy, of course."

"Hi there!" a girl behind the counter said. She had a mouthful of rainbow bands on her braces.

We greeted her, then scanned the menus.

"I'd like a medium frozen hot chocolate with whipped cream, please," I said. "I'm getting her order too."

The girl nodded, scribbling on a notepad.

Emery looked up at the menus one more time. "Can I have a medium hot chocolate, please?"

When we had our delicious-smelling drinks in hand, we headed out of Sweets.

"All right, here we go!" I said, ready to show Emery the beautiful campus. The only way to work on our relationship was to spend more time together. Otherwise, we'd stay strangers. Still, hanging out was weird. Everything felt so awkward, even after living together over the summer. Most of the time, we'd both been so busy with our own stuff that we'd barely seen each other. But I'd put on a brave face around Dad—trying to make him believe everything was good. That I was fine.

I hadn't even protested when Dad told me Emery had been accepted to Saddlehill and was joining me at school. It made me feel better about being away from home, honestly. This way, I wouldn't be jealous of Emery getting to spend so much free time with my dad.

"I'm ready," Emery said, smiling.

"I could get detention if the dean finds out I didn't give you a very thorough tour. That means I've got to run through a few basic and potentially boring facts about the school's history and reputation."

Emery laughed. "Go ahead. Honestly, I love history, so I doubt any of this will be boring."

That made me smile. She was obviously trying to make my job easy. "Awesome. So, Saddlehill Academy was founded in 1880 by Nathaniel and Elizabeth Thomas—two prominent Bostonians. There are just over one thousand students from grades six to twelve. The campus is plenty big enough to accommodate all the teachers, students, and staff who live here."

Emery nodded. "It doesn't feel crammed."

"As one of the top prep schools in the country, Saddlehill focuses on quality education. In addition, the school has a long, long history of graduates who have become famous models, actors, equestrians, soccer players, and practically every other neat job you could imagine."

"So, everyone is ultra-talented in, like, everything," Emery said, laughing. "Got it. I read the handbook over the summer. It got a bit overwhelming, though, to look at maps and stuff without actually being on campus."

"For sure. I think you'll get it all down much faster by walking around and learning where buildings are—such as that one, the activities department or AD." I pointed to the brick building with a tiny courtyard and a sprawling weeping willow.

"AD, got it," Emery said to herself.

"It's four floors of awesome," I explained. "You'll find snack and beverage bars and a movie theater. Oh, plus a gaming lounge with desktop computers and all kinds of systems."

"Sweet!" Emery said. "I brought my handheld system with me, but I want to play other stuff too. I love gaming."

"You do?" I didn't know how I'd missed her playing games.

"Yup. I love farming simulations and adventure games."

"I love games like those too! And horror games. Both ends of the spectrum."

We kept walking, and I turned and pointed down the campus. "That way? Academic buildings and the library."

"I wish the horses were here," Emery said, "because Bliss would love the front lawn. It's so picturesque."

Bliss was Emery's chestnut mare.

"So, *you* would love Bliss on the front lawn," I said, smiling.

"Yes." Emery burst into laughter. "What?" She grinned, shooting me side-eye. "You can't tell me you haven't had the same thought! With the buildings in the background, a horse on the lawn would be the perfect photo-shoot backdrop."

"Oh, I have definitely thought about it. Maybe we can sneak them over here somehow."

"I'm in," Emery said.

"But for now," I said, "Bliss will be happy at Foxbury."

"Hopefully, I will be too," Emery said quietly. "Happy there. And here, too."

"You're in great hands," I said. "Especially with riding. Rebecca's the best."

But as I thought about Emery training with Rebecca, a tiny stab of jealousy hit me. Everything had changed. *Everything.* I'd gone from not knowing this girl at all to living with her to coming to school with her, all within the past six months.

Plus, she'd spent a lot of time with my dad this summer. And had hung out even more with him last spring when I'd been away at school. I'd been here, at Saddlehill, watching her stories with pics of her going to the zoo with my dad and her mom. Or out at my and Dad's favorite Italian restaurant. Or having brunch at my house—my old house—before my dad and I had moved into hers.

"And," I added, taking a deep breath, "if you're ever feeling lonely or sad or anything, really, we have counselors. Plus, your resident advisor will be around a lot too, and they're usually so nice and friendly. Have you met yours yet?"

"I did, actually. He was really cool, and said he'll meet me in the common room to get to know each other soon. Have you met your RA?"

"Not yet," I said. "But I will in a bit. I'm glad you did, though. Are you okay with having a room to yourself this year?"

Emery half shrugged. "Kind of? I really wish new students could have roommates, but it probably won't be so bad. My mom was so happy about it. She said there would be plenty of other distractions this year."

"You're handling this way better than I did," I said. "Last year, I spent some serious time in the bathroom thinking I was going to barf. I was super anxious about starting classes and riding on the team, even though I wanted to come here more than anything."

"Really?" Emery's voice was soft. "You were that nervous?"

"Really. When my dad drove me here to drop me off, I

tried to tell him all the reasons we should turn around and go back home. I was convinced that everything was going to be scary and awful and not at all like what I'd imagined."

"And was it? Scary and awful, I mean?"

I smiled. "No. It was intense. The first week, especially, it was hard being away from home and my dad. But he was only a phone call away. It wasn't awful at all. And now it's almost weird going back to Fieldcrest."

"It is?"

"Very much. Saddlehill has become my home too. And, I don't know, but moving right before I went away to school didn't really help."

Emery frowned. She looked down at her hands, then back up at me. "I'm sorry. I can't imagine what that would feel like, honestly."

"Thanks, but it's not your fault." I paused, thinking. "Maybe it's for the best for me to leave my old house behind, you know? I have a lot of memories there, and some aren't so great. A fresh start might not be the worst thing in the world."

"That makes sense. It's kind of how I feel about leaving Bayview," Emery said. She held up a hand. "Not comparing that to anything you've gone through with your mom, of course. But a fresh start is kind of what I need too."

I tilted my head. What was she talking about? I racked my brain but couldn't think of any reason why Emery would want to get away from Bayview. Granted, we hadn't been friends before our parents had gotten together. So I wouldn't have heard about any drama going on there unless it had been big enough to spread through the entire stable. But I didn't press her on it, even though I was curious.

"It will be a fresh start for both of us," I said. "I know this"—I stopped and gestured around us, laughing—"is weird. But"—I took in a deep breath—"you can reach out if you need anything."

There. It wasn't an offer to hang out or spend all our time together. But if she felt alone or something was wrong, she could come to me if she needed to. Hopefully, she wouldn't need to, but I'd offered in case.

Instantly, I could see Emery relax. "Thank you, Abby. Really. Thanks a lot."

Side by side, we kept exploring, and I pointed out a few buildings as we walked.

"So, what do you think of it all?" I asked. "I know you did a prospective student tour, but any thoughts now?"

Emery drew her eyebrows together and was quiet for a few seconds. "Obviously, I toured the campus when I visited for my interview. But . . ." She paused. "Now I'm getting to see it as a student."

"And?"

"I like it. A lot. It's kind of weird, though. Not bad or anything. But weird to know I won't be going home tonight, and I'll be living here."

"I get it. I feel sort of like that now, and it's my second year. It gets better, though."

Hopefully, the awkwardness between us would get better too as we got to know each other. If not, it was going to be a *long* year.

Abby St. Clair, Tour Guide Extraordinaire

A S I CONTINUED TO SHOW EMERY around campus, I found myself enjoying it the more we talked and hung out. I led her down by the river, showing her the docks and the giant waterfront gazebo.

"When it's dark out, this whole place is lit up by fairy lights," I said, "and it looks so fantastic."

"I can't wait to see it! I have those kind of lights all over my room."

"We do too. Vivi and I both put some up, and it's so cozy in our room at night."

"Superbright lights sometimes give me anxiety," Emery said. "I know that sounds weird."

"Not at all, because they do the same thing to me."

The night Mom had left, I'd turned on every light in the house, scared to be alone in the dark. Now I couldn't stand ultrabright lights, because they took me right back to those hours when mine had been blazing while I waited for her to come home.

I started to invite Emery to come over to check out our lights sometime, but I stopped myself. I wasn't sure why, but it felt weird to invite her over. What if she didn't want to come and felt like she had to? Or what if she flat out said no thanks?

"Something that's giving me anxiety right now is my course load," Emery said.

"Well, how'd you do with summer homework? If you made it through that, you should be okay." I sipped my drink as I looked over at her.

"I didn't have any problems, thankfully. I kept up with all the required reading with no problem and got all my assignments done. I'll see my counselor after the first couple of weeks to update her on how I'm doing with everything."

I nodded. "That sounds good. I'm nervous too about classes,

but I also think our guidance counselors know what they're doing. Last year, I'd thought I for sure was going to be overwhelmed with some of my schoolwork, but it turned out okay."

"Whew. That helps to hear."

We passed the gazebo and started away from the gently flowing river—where we'd be coming for tonight's welcome-back party—and headed toward the heart of campus. Laughter rang out and excited voices carried over the campus as everyone was catching up with friends.

"Good," I said. "My best advice is to talk to your teachers if you have any problems. Mine were super helpful, and they seemed to really care about me—all of me—from the classroom to my extracurriculars."

That made Emery perk up a bit. "It'll be so nice to have teachers who take my riding seriously! No more penalties for missing a Friday class for a three-day show."

I nodded. "It's the best. So, what're you taking, anyway?"

"Let me see . . . ," Emery said, checking her phone. "Pre-algebra, English, a free study period, US history, Spanish, earth science, and gym."

Campus grew louder and busier as we walked back toward the buildings, sending little shivers of excitement through me.

I loved the atmosphere! The Saddlehill campus felt like a small city, with everything that I could possibly need in walking distance or by bus ride.

"Those sound good to me. I bet you'll have no problem. But hey, if you do? I *might* remember some of what I learned last year."

Emery laughed. "You got it. Thanks. How about you? What are you taking?"

I pulled up my schedule, which I'd decorated with colorful digital fall stickers. "Art, science, world history, English, Spanish, and Algebra I. I've got study hall in there too."

"That sounds intense," Emery said.

"A bit, maybe," I said. "I didn't *have* to take art this year, but I wanted to. I think I've got a good schedule overall."

"You really do," Emery said. "My mom was happy with my schedule. And so was your dad."

That twisting feeling in my chest returned.

"Oh, that's . . . cool," I said, kicking a rock off the sidewalk. *Cool?* Was that really the best response I had?

"He wanted to make sure I wasn't overwhelmed," she said.

"For sure." It was all I could muster. *Don't be a jerk,* I told myself. But I didn't know what else to say to Emery. This was weird. And hard. Maybe I needed a class or something on how to be a new stepsister. I didn't know how to stop being awkward.

"If only we could ride as long as we were in class every day," Emery said.

Now that was something I could roll with. *Whew.*

"Right?" I asked. "School feels like work, but riding never does to me, even though I practice endlessly."

"Oh, it's the same for me," Emery said. "But it's always worth the hours, especially when my mom and da—" Emery's cheeks flushed. "Erm, sorry, my mom and *your* dad come to my shows or practices and see me do well."

In that moment, I felt as though my chest cracked wide open. Like, actual bones were cracking and everything inside me was exposed for her to see.

I thought about how Natalie had told me the story about how she'd used an anonymous donor to have Emery, content to be a single mom until she'd met my dad. It was clear that Emery was excited to have a dad, but it didn't make this any easier on me.

I bit on the inside of my cheek to keep from crying. "Don't apologize," I said. "I knew what you meant." I felt like

I'd taken two punches: one, Emery saying *my mom and dad*, and two, when had Dad started going to her shows and practices? And why hadn't he ever mentioned it?

We walked in silence until I got an alert from my phone's calendar.

"Oh, shoot," I said. "I need to get to my RA meeting."

"No worries!" Emery said, almost a little too cheerfully.

"I have to get back, but I'll walk you to your dorm," I said. "I don't want you to get lost or anything."

Emery smiled. "I'm good, seriously. I can definitely find my way back to my dorm."

"You sure? I don't mind."

"Totally sure. Thank you for the tour." She raised her cup. "And the drink. I feel a lot better about this whole boarding-school thing."

Emery felt better about boarding school, but I felt worse about our situation. Our stepsister situation, specifically.

"You're welcome. If you're sure, then okay. I'll go, but I'll see you at the river party later."

With that, I gave Emery a small, awkward smile and headed down the sidewalk toward Amherst as the words we'd exchanged played on a loop in my brain.

Nice to Meet You

I TEXTED VIVI AS I WALKED.

Meet you in the common room!

Soon I'd reached Amherst, and I headed straight for the meeting. A few other students were already waiting, catching up and chatting with each other. They smiled at me when I walked in, then went back to their convos. The Amherst House common room had soft cottagecore vibes with tea-green love seats, a whitewashed fireplace, and lots of arched windows. Rustic bookcases held dozens of books and old-school board games. A door in the back led to an equally cozy screened porch.

"Hey," I said, snagging a seat and nodding to everyone.

Before we could get into a convo, an older girl walked into the room, brushing her black bangs from her eyes.

"Hi, hello! I'm Molly Fu," she said. "My pronouns are 'she' and 'her.' I'm your resident advisor, which you probably know from all the emails you got from me this summer. And the two I sent yesterday."

Laughing, I glanced around and realized Vivi hadn't shown up yet. Where was she?

Molly claimed an empty recliner, folding her legs under her. I couldn't help but eye the beautiful crown braid in her hair.

"Thanks for meeting me," Molly said. "I wanted to say hi and introduce myself before everyone got super busy with classes."

Vivi, cheeks pink, zipped through the doorway and squeezed in next to me on the sofa. I wanted to ask her where she'd been, but that was going to have to wait.

"So, a teensy bit about me," Molly said. "I'm a student here too, so I understand the pressures of attending a school like this. I wanted to be an RA because the person who most understood me was my own RA when I was your age."

I liked Molly already.

"I grew up with three siblings, so this feels right to me," Molly continued. "I'm not here to be your best friend. I know you've already got those. I *am* here to listen when you need someone and to offer advice should you need it. Okay?"

We all nodded, and I caught Joss Markham's eye. She smiled at me, and I waved. Joss started to wave back, but Selly noticed and her eyes burned into the side of Joss's head in a clear warning to stop being friendly with me. Joss ducked her head and didn't look back up.

Sigh. Not a total surprise after how Joss had been behaving toward the end of last year. She and I had been casual friends until she'd wanted to become Selly's and Nina's friend. Once she'd set her sights on those two, she'd ditched me. It looked like nothing was changing this year.

I still held out hope that Joss would see for herself that Selly was a terrible friend. My hope was dwindling, though.

"Let's go around the room, and everyone can introduce themselves," Molly said. "We all should have your pronouns on the house residents list, but if they've changed since you filled that out, let me know, okay?"

Everyone nodded, and Molly eyed me. "You can go first."

"I'm Abby St. Clair. I use 'she' and 'her,' and it's my second

~ 73 ~

year at Saddlehill. Riding is my number one focus, but I'm also interested in art. I'm not good at it. Yet. But I'm having fun learning."

Molly laughed. "I love art too. What's your favorite medium?"

"So far, sketching," I said. "But I want to try painting soon."

"Awesome!" Molly said. She nodded toward someone else. "You're up."

"I'm Zack Silva. My family and I immigrated here from Brazil when I was two. I'm a theater geek, and I want to be an actor. Oh, and I use they/them now."

Molly smiled at Zack. "Cool, noted! I'll update the list. I immigrated to the US when I was just a bit older than you. Do you ever go back to visit Brazil?"

"Every year!" they said, nodding.

It was Selly's turn next. She flipped her chestnut-brown hair over her shoulder. "I'm Selly Hollis, and I use 'she' and 'her.' I'm a rider, and I love my horse, Ember. I'm going to be an Olympic equestrian one day."

"Sweet!" Molly said. "I rode horses as a kid, but Western. Not English. They're pretty different, right?"

"Very," Selly said dryly. She shook her head, almost as if

she couldn't believe Molly didn't know every single difference between the two. The horror!

I sighed. Selly's attitude had always sucked. She was convinced she was a better rider than everyone else. And okay, she wasn't wrong about her dressage skills. I could give her that. But her time as the top rider on our team was over.

It didn't take too long to finish going around the rest of the room and introducing ourselves.

"Thank you all for hanging with me," Molly said. "I'm so glad I got to see you all face-to-face. I'll let you go in case you want to keep unpacking or get ready for tonight's welcome-back party at the river."

We murmured our thanks, and everyone started trickling out of the common room.

I turned to Vivi. "Did you get lost between our room and here?" I asked.

She snorted. "Ha, ha, Abs. I just lost track of time."

Vivi headed for the door, but I hurried to sidle up next to her. "Try again."

"Whaaaat?" Vivi asked.

"You always do that when you're lying!" I said, grinning as I pointed this out to her.

"Nooo!" Vivi rubbed a hand over her face.

"Yeesss. You stretch out your words just like that! It's a tell."

Vivi rolled her eyes, and we headed upstairs to our room. Once we were inside, I shut the door and stared at her.

"I can be very annoying," I said. "I'm just going to keep bugging you until you tell me."

"You really can be *very* annoying," Vivi said. She smiled, though. "Fine!"

I sat on the chaise lounge, waiting for her to start talking.

"I might have been texting Asher, and he *might* have said he's looking forward to seeing me tonight."

"WHAT?" I half yelled. "Why would you keep that a secret? That's *amazing*, Vivi! Tell me everything!"

Asher Barnes was a supercute, supersweet guy in our grade. He rode, too, which was even cooler. But he was a brand-new beginner rider, so we didn't have lessons together.

Vivi grinned. "You know we've been talking, like, all summer."

"And?" I prompted.

"And we started texting back and forth while you were out with Emery. I kind of forgot what time it was and didn't check my phone right away when I got the reminder about meeting with Molly."

I grinned.

"What?" Vivi asked.

"Oh, nothing. This is cute, that's all."

"You know what's not cute?" Vivi pouted. "The fact that I have nothing to wear tonight. Help me?"

"Absolutely!"

Vivi put on an upbeat playlist, and we dove into our boxes of clothes.

"How'd it go hanging with Emery?" Vivi raised an eyebrow.

"It was fine."

"Fine? What happened?"

"Well, she said something weird. She said my dad's been coming to her shows and practices. I had no idea. None. He's never said a word about it."

Vivi frowned. "That is weird."

"We've always had different practices and competed in different classes at shows since Emery was a rating lower than me. And now, of course, I started thinking about all the recent practices and shows my dad's missed of mine. I know how this sounds, but I hope it's not because he was at Emery's."

"I hope he wasn't either. Are you going to ask him?"

I shrugged. "Maybe at some point? But not yet."

Vivi gave me a supportive smile. "Understandable. I'm sure you'll find the right time to talk to him."

I knew if it continued to bother me, I'd have to. But I really, really didn't want to. Even the thought of bringing it up to my dad felt uncomfy and made me feel anxious. I didn't want to be the insecure, jealous girl I was turning into!

"Hopefully. But right now? I want to focus on tonight and having fun."

"I'm so in!"

And with that, we started tossing outfit options onto her bed. Sure, it was a bit early to get ready, but we *had* to look amazing!

I Do Believe
in Unicorns

OKAY, THESE ARE DEFINITELY THE
outfits," I said, looking in the full-length mirror
at the colorful sundresses we'd put on over our
bathing suits.

"Totally agree," Vivi said.

Carrying our beach towels, we headed out of Amherst,
our flip-flops smacking the sidewalk as we headed to the
riverbank at the back of campus.

"At least it won't be dark for a while, so we still have
plenty of time to swim if we want," Vivi said.

Swimming in the river was strictly prohibited after sunset.

"Definitely. I hope there's an empty raft that we can snag. Then we can float and have a soda."

"Perfect," Vivi said. "I need food first, though."

"Me too. Like, multiple hot dogs."

Vivi's phone buzzed, and she checked it, a smile coming quickly to her face.

"Let me guess . . . Asher?"

"Yup. He said he's at the riverbank, and he asked if I wanted him to save me a seat on his blanket."

"What did you say?"

"I said, 'Sure!' with an exclamation point and a smiley face."

"Perfect."

"You cool if I hang out with him a bit?" Vivi asked.

"Absolutely. As long as you tell me everything after."

We started down the gentle slope of the hill to the riverbank. The hillside was already covered with beach towels and folding chairs as students had claimed their spots in the grass. I inhaled, taking in the deliciously smoky scent of charcoal.

"I'm going to look for him," Vivi said. "Meet you later?"

"For sure! Have fuuun!" I said in a singsong voice.

She rolled her eyes but tossed me a smile before we mixed into the crowd. I shook my head, wondering how she did it. She was always so calm around her crushes. I was the opposite, with zero chill and lots of blushing. I'd tried talking to a cute girl at my old stable last summer, and I'd bumbled every single word. The embarrassing scene still played in my brain sometimes.

At the banquet tables with rows and rows of food, I spotted Thea, grabbed a plate, and got in line next to her.

"We're totally grabbing floats and getting in the river, right?" she asked me.

"You know it. Let's eat and then go get rafts."

It didn't take long for me to load a paper plate with two hot dogs, barbecue chips, and a soft, oversized chocolate chip cookie. Food and drink in hand, I headed for the dock and found a place to sit with my feet dangling over the water. Thea sat next to me, sniffing in my direction.

"You smell like coconut," she said. "It reminds me of the beach, and now I want to go."

"Maybe the weekend after next? I've been wanting to take Beau there anyway. He needs so much work around water—I thought it would be a good place to go before it's too cold."

"I'm in. We can text Maia to see if she or any of the other older riders are free to take us."

The horse-friendly part of the nearby beach was the best. It was an easy twenty-minute walk on horseback from the stable. We weren't allowed to go without chaperones, but Maia and her friends were old enough to take us younger riders.

"Chaos could use some conditioning too," Thea said. "He's had such a relaxed summer that he needs the extra work before he gets a serious hay belly. And that's in addition to lessons."

"Beau's had a lot of time off from hard-core practices. Maybe we should start getting up and hacking them before school? We could hit the hills around the stable and work on getting them in better shape over the next few weeks."

"Getting up any earlier sounds like the absolute worst," Thea said. "But also, exactly what Chaos could use. I need a few days to adjust to being back in school, but we could start the week after next."

"Sounds like a plan. I'll even bring us coffee."

"I'm keeping you," Thea said. "Forever."

"You better."

We gobbled our food, and I spotted Selly, Nina, and Joss all clustered together on a hot-pink beach towel. I wished Thea and I could eat with Joss and show her there were nicer people to hang out with than Selly, but there was no way she'd ditch Selly to come with us.

"Joss, huh?" Thea asked in a low voice.

"It's hard to see someone so nice hanging out with people so awful. Joss could do much better than Nina and Selly. Why she chooses to hang out with them, I'll never know."

"I don't know either. All we can do is be nice to her on the rare occasions Nina and Selly let her spend five minutes with us. Maybe she'll see how it can be to have decent friends."

I wiped my salty fingers on my napkin. "Maybe. Unless, of course, Selly and Nina pull her even deeper into their circle and they become a trio of evil. Which I could totally see happening."

Thea grimaced. "Same. It sucks because Nina was fine last year until she became superglued to Selly. And then those two?"

"Became double trouble," I said.

"Like, full-on Team Rocket."

I laughed. "But way less entertaining."

"And sans cool outfits," Thea said.

"Or a great motto."

We both laughed.

"Now they're slowly pulling in Joss," I said. "And, I'm not going to lie, I'm worried about Emery."

"Why?"

Together, we stood and headed to throw away our trash. We weaved our way up the bank, careful not to step on anyone's blankets or beach towels.

"I don't want them to pull her in too. It's just like them to befriend her to bother me."

"Oh, definitely."

I sighed as we made our way over to a pile of floats, pool noodles, and rafts. "Maybe they'll focus on Joss and not even notice Emery."

I hated saying that, but it would be better than the alternative: Nina and Selly befriending Emery. I didn't have any reason to think Emery would suddenly morph into a mean girl, but she was new here. That came with its own kinds of pressure. And that might make her more vulnerable than she'd normally be.

"I hope so," Thea said. "Those two are smart. And sneaky. They could befriend Emery before she even realizes it."

"I know. That's exactly what I'm afraid of."

Thea and I looked at each other for a second, both of us taking a deep breath at the same time.

"Well, all we can do is hope for the best," Thea said.

And prepare for the worst, I thought. But I kept that to myself as I bent down to pick up a blue foam raft.

"Abby, forget these rafts," Thea said. "Look!"

I followed her gaze down the river and in the direction of where she'd pointed.

"Oh. My. God," I said.

With small squeals, we took off toward another dock a few yards away, where a couple of adults were blowing up inflatable floats. I couldn't take my eyes off two giant golden-horned white unicorns with rainbow manes and tails.

"Let's grab those!" Thea said.

We waited not so patiently for one of the teachers—I think he was a high school math teacher—to finish filling the floats with air and clip them onto a long rope tethered to the dock. Then we stripped down to our bathing suits and left our clothes in a pile on top of our flip-flops. I waded up to my knees into the river, then managed to climb onto my unicorn without tipping it or falling off the other side and lowered myself into the center.

Grinning, I looked over at Thea as she launched herself into the middle of her float, laughing the entire time as she got settled. Lazily, I steered my float closer to Thea's. Once we were nearly bumping into each other, I leaned my head back and closed my eyes.

This was perfection. The scent of charcoal and grilled burgers wafted over me, and even though I was stuffed, I took an appreciative sniff.

"It doesn't get much better than this," Thea said. "It's helping me forget that school starts on Monday, and it's going to be the busiest week ever."

"The weekend show coming up definitely doesn't help. On one hand, I'm glad it gives me something else to focus on besides school. On the other hand, you just said it—it's the first week back and there's so much to do."

"There is, but I know we'll get through it," Thea said.

I opened my eyes and looked over at Thea, my eye catching on the bright blue of her bathing suit, which matched one of the blue stripes in the unicorn's mane.

"All I want is a good show season. One that's *way* better than last year's."

"I bet it will be. Fieldcrest was a fluke, Abs."

"What if it wasn't?" I shook my head. "I didn't do any better at regionals!"

"You didn't fall!"

I groaned. "That cannot be my bar. Not falling. The Fieldcrest Classic wrecked my confidence so hard that I let it carry over to regionals. And yeah, I didn't fall, but I choked. I didn't finish well enough to even come close to getting to nationals."

"It was a tough season for you. There was so much going on with your dad and Emery. I don't blame you for not being your best."

I shot Thea a small smile. "Thanks, ugh. But I can't blame them. It was my fault. I got in my own head."

"It's a new season," Thea said, "and if there's anything I can do to help, just tell me."

"You got it. More than anything, I want to work on conditioning Beau and getting him less spooked around water."

Thea skimmed a hand along the top of the water. "Lucky for you, it's gonna be hot out for a while. So we can get that beach trip in like we talked about. Maybe bring him down to the river, too. Ooh, and we can crank up a hose and have a water fight!"

"You're *so* on for all of those! Oh, and remind me later to send you an article by Lauren Towers that I was reading on

HeartHorse. She wrote about how she had to overcome serious jumping anxiety when she was around our age after a bad fall."

Lauren Towers was another Canterwood Crest success story. She was a little younger than Sasha, and like the other girl, she'd come to Canterwood from Briar Creek, Sasha's old stable in Union, Connecticut. There was something in that city's water supply, I swear. It kept producing superstar equestrians!

"Oh, really? The way she rides now, you'd never know."

"Right? It makes her feel more relatable. And like overcoming this phobia of Beau's is possible."

"Speaking of Lauren, did you see that post on Instagram? She just posted the cutest pic of her with her old mare, Whisper. They're seriously the most adorable."

"Nooo! I saw the one of her trying a new tea. I'll have to look later."

Where Sasha's Insta showed off her go-to lip glosses and beauty products, Lauren's was all about teas. I'd tried a bunch of her recs and was already starting to build a tiny collection of her faves that I liked.

I sighed, feeling a bit more content now. Just like that, Thea helped me believe that maybe, just maybe, everything would be okay.

Students, Assemble

WAY TOO EARLY THE NEXT morning, Emery and I headed to Assembly. Vivi had left a few minutes before me because she'd needed to call her mom this morning, so she'd opted to do so on her walk, and I'd promised to meet up with her in front of Harwich Auditorium after Assembly.

Emery and I stifled yawns as we walked in the quiet early morning. Campus was crawling with students. It was almost painfully obvious which students were new and which were returning. The newbies stared at their phones, wide-eyed and likely looking at the campus maps. The returning students meandered across campus, walking with more confidence in their steps.

"I'm strangely nervous about this," Emery said. "It feels like I'm the one getting up in front of the entire school to speak."

"I'm kind of nervous too. But I think it's more the realization that school's about to start, and this is our last day of freedom. Even though I love school, the last day of summer is still hard."

Emery nodded. "That makes sense."

"But in less than an hour, we'll be out of there," I said.

Emery yawned again. "Remind me why we had to get up early on a Sunday? This couldn't be a noon assembly?"

"Right? Seriously. At least we have the rest of the day to do whatever."

Emery nodded. "Good point."

All around us, students made their way up the various winding sidewalks to reach the auditorium. The gigantic building could hold hundreds of students at once and was one of the largest on campus. Once inside, Emery and I snagged the first pair of empty seats we saw.

"Wow," Emery said. "This place is amazing. It almost

makes me want to get into theater just to be able to stand on that stage."

"Me too! The drama students do put on some great productions."

Rich red velvet curtains made the room feel dramatic, along with hundreds and hundreds of deep-cushioned seats and rope lights along the floor. Low lights lit up the stage, and a spotlight was trained on a microphone and podium at center stage.

Everyone fell silent when Dean Paulson made his way up onstage, stopping at the podium. The dean had one of those faces—kind but intimidating. He lifted the mic from the podium and, with a smile, walked up near the front of the stage.

"Welcome, students and faculty, to the beginning of another year at Saddlehill Academy," Dean Paulson said. "I am so pleased to see all of you here!" His gaze shifted from section to section of the auditorium.

I shifted back into my seat, fighting the urge to check my phone as the dean kept talking. But I did not want detention before school had even started.

"Each of us here—from students to faculty—represents this institution," Deal Paulson said. "We do not tolerate a lax attitude toward our school rules and values."

I shivered a bit in my seat, as if I'd done something wrong. The dean's voice made me feel as if he were speaking directly to me in a stern way, even though he wasn't.

Thankfully, the speech flew by, and the dean didn't drone on for too long.

"With all of that said, I welcome you as this year's students of Saddlehill Academy," Dean Paulson said. "Let's make this another wonderful year!"

Emery and I clapped along with the entire student body. I was grateful not to be in her place as a newbie. Last year had been tough. It had taken me almost to the end of the school year to learn how to balance classes, a social life, and riding.

Everyone clapped until Dean Paulson was off the stage, and then people started filing out of the auditorium. I darted into the aisle when there was a gap in students. Emery fell behind me, but she waved for me to go ahead. The girls she'd met at the riding team meeting—Wren and Zoe—had found her.

Outside the auditorium, I checked my texts—specifically, the group chat with Vivi, Thea, and a couple of our other friends. Last night we'd been texting about meeting up after the assembly.

Thea: Want to meet at the cafeteria for brunch?

Abby: Yes, def! See you there.

Even though Vivi was now beside me and also on her phone, I asked her, "Brunch at the caf with everyone?"

"Definitely," she said. "I need some caffeine after that welcome-back speech."

"Oh, same. We know we're always representing Saddle-hill in—"

"Everything we do," Vivi finished. "And we've got an image to uphold."

"Or else . . ." I made a throat-slashing motion.

Vivi and I walked across the campus, careful to stay on the sidewalks and not step on the pristine grass. Too many students had been met with demerits for that kind of "devious" behavior.

Inside the caf, Vivi and I got our food, and we weaved our way through the crowded room and headed for our usual table near the back of the room. It was the best because it sat near one of the arched windows and sunlight poured inside, causing me to stretch and soak it in. It felt *so* good to be back. And, in this moment, I felt more confident than ever that it was going to be a great year.

Blabby Abby

HIII!" I SAID, SPOTTING A COUPLE OF Vivi's and my friends.

"Hey!" Willa Hunt, another seventh grader, said as she stood and waited for me to put down my tray so we could hug.

"Your new haircut," I said, grinning at her, "is fantastic."

Willa smiled back, running a hand over her short dark blond hair, which was cropped on top with shaved sides. "Thank you. I finally went for it, and this is the hair I've always wanted but was too afraid to try."

"You look like a high-fashion model," I said. Sliding my tray next to Willa, I sat down by her. We'd become friends in math class last year, and she was a beginner equestrian. Next to Willa was her bestie, Ankita Batra, whom I also really liked.

"I only hit my snooze button six times this morning," Ankita said. "Anyone else?"

Most of the group raised their hands. Vivi didn't raise hers, so I reached over and raised it for her, which made everyone laugh.

"I'm so glad to see you all," Ankita said. "I missed your faces this summer!"

"Me too," I said. "Texting is not the same as hanging out."

"Guess who Willa ran to hang out with first?" Ankita asked, smiling and bumping her shoulder against Willa's.

"*Stop,*" Willa said. "I did not!"

"Did too," Ankita said. "You didn't even unpack!"

"Spill," Vivi said.

"Tell us!" I added.

Willa blushed three shades of pink but smiled. "Fiiine. I went to see Quinn."

"Ooh," I said. "Did you two talk more this summer?"

When Willa and I had texted during summer break, she'd

told me there was a girl she liked, but she didn't know if the other girl liked her back.

Willa nodded. "Almost every day. She's really smart, really funny, and *really* sweet."

I grinned along with the rest of my friends. "This is so cute," I said.

"Seriously, so adorable," Vivi said.

"Stop it, omigod," Willa said. But she was all smiles. "We might study together later in the week."

"You're so lucky!" I said. "No cute people for me this summer."

Thea pouted. "Not a single person?"

I shook my head. "I'd hoped I'd see this girl again at my old stable, but she must have been on vacation or something this summer."

"Don't worry," Willa said, patting my shoulder. "We'll find you someone cute."

"What about the fall harvest dance?" Vivi asked. "Are we all going together, then? Or are you asking Quinn, Willa?"

The fall harvest dance in mid-September was The Event that got me in the mood for autumn. It was pumpkin spice central! Everything was fall-themed, from the drinks to the desserts to the decor. It felt like stepping into one of those Hallmark movies I caught on TV sometimes. The very, very fall-themed ones with people falling in love at the pumpkin patch or saving the family orchard from the grips of an evil out-of-town investor.

"That sounds like so much pressure," Willa said. "I'd like to go as a group, but if Quinn's open to a dance or two, I'm in."

"Sounds good to me, too," I said. "I can't wait. It's going to be so much fun. I have no idea what I'm wearing, so I'll need to go shopping."

"I'm down to hit the mall soon," Vivi said.

"Let's definitely go next week," Ankita said. "Right now, I'm swamped getting my room set up and fielding ten phone calls a day from my parents."

My eyes widened. "Ten? Why ten?"

She twirled a sweet potato fry in the air. "They miss me, apparently. A lot! Even though I was here last year, they seemed to have a harder time dropping me off this year."

"How rude of them to miss you," I said in mock indignation.

"I know, right?" Ankita said. "But it should get better in a few days."

"Hopefully," Vivi said, shaking her head. "I couldn't talk to my parents that much every single day."

Almost as if on cue, my phone buzzed. "If that's my dad wanting to talk," I joked, "then he's totally set up spyware on my phone and has been listening to us."

I looked at the screen, seeing a new text notification from an unknown number. I rolled my eyes. "Aw, my dad isn't spying on me," I said. "It's a spam text."

"Boo," Vivi said. "C'mon, Mr. St. Clair, what are you doing respecting Abby's privacy like that?"

"Right?" I asked, laughing as I swiped my thumb over the new text, preparing to delete it.

Much yikes, it said.

Um, okay?

Maybe it wasn't spam; it was a wrong number.

My friends laughed at something Ankita said, but their voices were all background noise to me. I was too focused on my phone to hear them clearly.

That was when I noticed something: the text hadn't been sent to just me. It had gone to several numbers I didn't recognize and a few that were in my contacts.

Selly.

Emery.

Keir.

Nina.

Thea.

And a few other riders who were sometimes in my lessons with my main group.

Selly: Who is this?

Keir: Did someone get a new #?

Someone had clearly changed their number, because who else would group text me and some of my friends? If it was a wrong number, it would just be sent to one of us. Right? Or it would come to me and all spam numbers I didn't know. But neither of those things had happened. I went to close out of the text when a new notification popped up.

I blinked at my phone, then shut my eyes for a full three seconds before opening them again. Group name changed to Blabby Abby.

"Abby?" I heard Vivi say my name, but it was as if I were underwater. Her voice sounded garbled and far away.

Blabby Abby? Who was messing around? White-hot panic flashed through my body and made me hot and cold at the same time. What if . . . what if someone *knew*? What if they knew what I did to Selly? And they were going to tell everyone? *Stop*, I told myself. *You're being way too paranoid. No one knows.*

"Sorry," I said to everyone. "Just got a weird group text."

Okay, ha, ha, who is this? I texted the group.

You haven't "blabbed" anything, I reminded myself. So it was most definitely a joke.

A video appeared below my text with a shocked emoji.

"Everything okay, Abby?" Ankita asked, concern in her voice. "I didn't get a text."

But I didn't answer her. Instead, I tapped on the video. Anxiety and curiosity twisted my stomach. I had no idea what this could possibly be.

The video started, and it was a shaky view of a wooden wall. A stall wall. Then it zoomed in on someone. Someone who looked awfully familiar.

"I know I've done nothing but complain to you about Emery, but she's actually . . . awful," said my voice on the video.

Blood pounded in my ears. My friends went still and silent as they listened to my voice coming from my phone, and out of the corner of my eye, I could see them all looking at me. Their curious looks felt like burns to my skin, and it was as if I'd forgotten how to breathe.

"She's . . . a spoiled kid with an evil stepmother who hates me and is out to steal my dad."

I was saying those things.

I was the voice.

I was the girl on camera.

But those weren't my words! I mean, yes, they were, but words were missing!

"Abby," Vivi started, but she fell silent when Video Abby started talking again.

"She's a better rider than I am . . . I need to work . . . harder on my own skills," I said on the video.

The video shifted from the ground to zooming in through the iron bars on Beau's stall. I came into sharp focus with an arm wrapped around his neck.

Then the video ended.

My hands shook so hard, I could barely hold my phone. Another new text came in. This one was just to me.

Unknown sender: This is only the start, Abby! 😊 xoxo, the Truth X. Poser

Then another text. This time from Rebecca.

Don't forget to take Emery on a ride today!

Rebecca had asked me yesterday to go riding with Emery

today, but I couldn't even deal with that right now. Without replying to my riding coach, I shut off my phone. I didn't want to see anyone reply to the video. My friends, who were also my classmates and fellow riders, all saw that. Saw a video of me trash-talking Emery.

Except I hadn't. But who would believe that when they had video "proof" in front of them?

And what did the sender mean, *This is only the start*? What else did they have on me? I tried to take a deep breath, but I couldn't.

"Um," I said, standing. "I've got to go."

I couldn't even see through my tears. There were black spots in my vision, almost as if I were going to faint.

"Abby, wait," Vivi said, reaching for me. "Don't—"

But I didn't stick around to let her finish.

Gulping uneven breaths, I took off for Amherst House. I needed to shut myself away in my room and hide from everyone. For a long, *long* time.

Supersleuth Mode: Activated!

SOMEONE KNOCKED ON MY DOOR. "GO away!" I croaked.

"Abby, it's me," Vivi said through the door. "I was just knocking to let you know I'm coming in, okay?"

The door opened, and my roommate walked inside. I swiped my hand across my eyes, but I couldn't stop crying. Vivi's arms were around me before I could even get a word out. She squeezed me tight, letting me cry. Finally, after what felt like forever, I let go of her and tried to take a deep breath.

"I didn't say those things!" I said, my voice shaking. "I told

Beau how Emery *isn't* a total jerk with a horrible mom. God, I don't even *secretly* believe any of those things!"

Vivi nodded. "I believe you, Abby. I know you don't think any of those things about her."

But Vivi didn't even know the rest of the story. The huge secret I'd been keeping from everyone. Even my best friends. The secret I had to make sure stayed buried. The one I had a sick feeling this person knew.

"So why would someone film me and edit it to make it sound like I hated Emery?" I wiped tears off my cheeks.

"I don't know," Vivi said. "It's an awful thing to do, and obviously it's something to hurt you."

"And ruin my relationship with Emery." I groaned. "We're never going to get past our awkward stage now. Never. No way will she believe me."

"You have to talk to her," Vivi said.

I shook my head. "What am I going to say? 'Emery, don't believe that video. It's fake'? She won't believe that. I don't know if *I* would believe that." Fresh tears made my eyes blur. "And what about everyone on that group text? And all our friends who watched me play that video? They're all going to think I'm some whiny brat who can't cope with having a new stepsister."

"They'll believe you if you talk to them," Vivi said. "Abs, it's the only option. It's the *best* option."

"False. Hiding out in our room for the rest of the year is my only option."

Vivi raised an eyebrow. "No way. Nope. I'm not going to let you do that. The year just started, and it's going to be amazing. This video is clearly a fake, and we'll prove it."

"How?"

"We're going to figure out who did this," Vivi said, giving me a single nod. "Then we'll make them come clean and tell everyone the truth."

More than that, I had to get to them and make them stop before they exposed my secret. I didn't want any more hints coming out about what I'd done.

"How are we going to do that?" I asked. "It could have been anyone."

Vivi shook her head. "No, it couldn't have been. We'll go full-on detective mode. We'll make a list of suspects and their possible motives. We'll start asking around and find out who was at the barn that day."

For the first time since I'd seen the video, a bit of hope stirred in my chest. "You'll really help me do all that?"

"Of course," Vivi said. "You're my best friend. Someone hurt you, and we're going to find out who. I promise."

Vivi was so willing to help me, it made guilt feel heavy in my chest. For a half second, I considered telling her what I'd done to Selly, but I couldn't bring myself to say the words. I couldn't stand to have my best friend look at me any differently than she did now.

Instead, I said, "Thank you. I don't know how we'll figure this out, though. There are so many people who could have come in and out of the stable. I mean, really, who does this to someone? Isn't spying on a person and filming them against the law?!"

Vivi winced. "If it's not, it should be. First thing we're going to do, though, is you have to give me your phone. I'm going to write down that unknown phone number, and tonight we can dig around online to see if we can find anyone tied to it."

I dug my phone from where I'd stuffed it under my pillow. I handed it to Vivi, and she powered it on. For a second, I thought about how she'd see the other text to me from the anon number. But it didn't say anything incriminating, so I didn't care.

"Passcode?" she asked. I told her, and she nodded. "I'm in."

"What's everyone saying?" I asked. "I didn't want to know before, but now I'm kind of dying that I don't know."

Vivi opened the group text and scanned it for a second. "No one has said anything mean. Except Selly, and she didn't say anything, exactly. She just left a laughing emoji."

"Of course she did. So everyone else was silent?" I groaned. "That means they believe the video, and they all think I'm pathetic for talking crap about Emery."

"Stop." Vivi made a slashing motion with her hand. "I'm on it. Just zip it for a minute."

I listened to her while she started typing, trying not to let my thoughts run too wild. *You'll figure this out,* I told myself. *Vivi's not going anywhere, and she wants to help you. So, let her.*

After a couple of minutes, Vivi looked up from my phone and took a breath. "All right. Here's what I want to send to everyone in that group: 'Hey! I'm sorry someone sent you all that video of me. It was a fake—someone edited it to make it sound like I was saying horrible things about Emery and her mom. I know it looks and sounds one way in the video, but lots of words are missing. I'm going to figure out who the Mysterious Sender is, and until I do, I hope you'll believe me.'" Vivi stopped reading and looked up at me. "What do you think?"

"That's so perfect," I said. "Wow, yeah, I wouldn't have been able to put together a halfway decent text right now, let alone something that good. I'm still . . ."

"Shocked?" Vivi asked.

"Definitely."

"I'm glad you like it. I'm going to send it then, okay?"

I nodded. "Yes, please."

"I'm also going to mute any replies to it for now," Vivi said. "You can unmute when you're ready, but if it were me, I'd want it that way until I felt like talking or responding."

"You're an actual lifesaver."

Vivi handed me my phone. "Now, you've got to do the hard part."

"Throw my phone out the window?" I asked.

"Ha, try again."

I shook my head. "I don't want to!"

"Abby, you *have* to text Emery!" Vivi exclaimed.

"I have to do more than text her," I said. "Rebecca wants me to take her on a ride today. A 'welcome' ride around the property."

Vivi smiled. She actually *smiled*. "That's perfect."

"No, it's not!"

"Yes, it is," Vivi said. "You get to see her right away and tell her what happened. This way, you won't be sitting in your room agonizing over what she thinks or how she's going to react when you talk to her."

"You forget that sitting in my room and agonizing is part of who I am," I said, fully aware that I was whining. "I need time to prepare and think."

"And worry and torment yourself?" Vivi shook her head. "Uh-uh. No. This is really good. Text her now and get it over."

I frowned. "You're very bossy right now."

"And very right," Vivi said. "Do it. C'mon. You got this, Abs."

"Fiiine. I'll text her now. She probably won't even respond."

I sat still for a minute, lost in thought about what to say. Then, finally, I started typing.

Hey! First, I want to say I'm so, so sorry for that video. I'd like to explain in person. Rebecca wants us to ride together today, so when are you free? I didn't say what the video makes you think I said, btw. I promise. Lmk when you want to meet.

I read it aloud to Vivi, and she nodded her approval.

"Sent," I said. "She's never going to write me back. She's

probably on the phone with her mom and my dad, telling them about it."

My stomach lurched. But instead of crying, I got up and mixed some plant food into water and gave it to my plants who needed it. It was all I could do not to start crying again. Then my phone vibrated.

Emery: 1 hour?

"One hour question mark," I said. "That's all Emery wrote. Oh my god, she hates me."

"Text her back before you change your mind," Vivi said.

My best friend was the worst today! I groaned and texted Emery. Sounds good. Meet you at the stable!

"Now I have one hour to freak out," I said. "Ugh."

Vivi shook her head. "No. You have one hour to walk me through the entire convo you had with Beau, get dressed, and meet Emery."

I took a deep breath and told Vivi everything. Well, *mostly* everything.

Nothing but the Truth... *Almost*

AN HOUR LATER I STOOD OUTSIDE THE stable. I still wasn't convinced that Emery was actually going to show up. The sun warmed my bare arms, and I shaded my eyes with my hand as I looked around the stable yard in case Emery had gotten here before me. But I didn't see her.

Vivi and I had talked right up until the moment I'd left to grab one of the frequent buses here. We hadn't come up with any solid suspects who could have possibly spied on me and leaked a doctored video, but I also wasn't in the clearest of headspaces yet. I felt violated. My privacy had been stripped from me, and someone had not only filmed me without my consent, but they'd spent time editing my words. Deleting my words. Making me sound as if I hated my new stepsister and her mom. *But as horrified as you are, think how Emery feels,* I reminded myself.

And I couldn't even begin to think too much about what would happen if the rest of my secret ever came out. Right now, I had to focus on Emery.

I shifted from one paddock-boot-clad foot to the other. The sun was still hot, and it was sticky out—a typical New England summer day. Sweat prickled along my hairline. This might have been one of the longest waits of my life. But I would hang out here until Emery showed. Or didn't. I checked my phone. Nothing.

And then I saw her.

Emery, arms wrapped across her chest, marched toward me, her lips pressed together and her eyes red.

Awesome. I'd made her cry. On her first weekend at Saddlehill. *Way to go, Abby,* I told myself.

"Hi, um, thanks for meeting me," I said.

"I probably wouldn't have come, honestly," Emery said.

"But Rebecca followed up and wanted to make sure we were riding together, so here I am."

Ouch. I winced.

"I get it. You have every right to be mad at me."

Emery started for the stable, and I hurried to keep up with her. Her arms were at her sides now, fists clenched.

"Emery, wait," I said. "Please, can we just talk for a minute before we—"

"We don't need to talk," she snapped. "I think you've said enough lately. Like, plenty."

"It wasn't like that!" I reached for Emery's wrist, trying to slow her down. She spun around to face me, cheeks reddening. She sucked in a breath, and before she could yell at me, I kept going. "I know we haven't known each other long. I get that you have no reason to trust me. But I promise—the video was doctored. The words were mine, yes, but a *lot* of words were missing too. Let me tell you exactly what I said, please."

Emery snorted. "That sounds really, really convenient, Abby."

"I know. I get it. But it's so easy to fake videos and alter audio. I can do that on at least two apps. Can't you?"

She stared at me, tilting her head a bit. "Yeah. I guess

I can. But maybe you did that. Maybe you made the video somehow and sent it out as a way to let everyone know how you really feel about me."

"Why? To humiliate myself? Do you have any idea how that made me look to my friends? The people on our riding team?"

"Do you have any idea how it made *me* look?" She was yelling now. "I'm the target of a video that makes it sound like I'm some awful stepsister with a horrible, evil stepmom. Everyone here knows you. They don't know me, so they're definitely going to think it's true!"

"They won't," I said. "I've already started telling everyone the truth: the video was edited. Can I tell you, too? Please?"

Emery stared at me, teeth clenched. I desperately wanted her to let me explain. Just for a moment.

Finally, she shrugged. "Okay. Tell me."

So I did. Keeping my eyes on hers, I told her word for word what I'd said to Beau, minus my worry about the secret of mine the Truth X. Poser (or as I'd started to think of them, the TXP) might know. Thankfully, her anger seemed to deflate a bit with my words. I could see it all over her face—she was trying to decide if she could trust me. If she could trust my words over video evidence to the contrary.

"So, yes, I talked to Beau about you," I said. "But not at all what the video made it sound like." I paused, thinking about how to phrase the next part. "And they texted me and said it wasn't the end. So I'm guessing they're going to keep harassing me."

There. That wasn't a lie.

The slight frown on Emery's face relaxed some. "It's hard, you know? There's a video that looks and sounds so real."

"I know, I know. I would have a hard time believing me too. But honestly, have you felt *any* of that sort of energy from me? Bad vibes, like I didn't like you or your mom?"

Emery shook her head. "No. No, I haven't. That's why it hurt so much, I think. Because so far, you've gone out of your way to be nice to me, and you seemed to like my mom."

"I do," I said. "It hasn't been easy. For either of us. I know I'm awkward around you, but I'm not out to get you. Someone—and I don't know who—wants to mess up our relationship."

And ruin me at school and the stable, I thought.

"But why?"

"I don't know. But Vivi and I are going to figure it out."

"You are?" Emery twisted the silver ring on her pointer finger before looking up at me.

"Yes. We're going to make a list of everyone who could

have possibly done this. Then we're going to start digging. Vivi's so furious that someone did this to me—and to you, to be honest—that she's a step away from busting out a magnifying glass and a tweed detective hat."

Emery cracked a smile. "That's a good best friend."

"She really is. I promise you, I wouldn't waste her time trying to help figure this out if it weren't real."

"Fine," Emery said, blowing out a breath. "I'm going to trust you on this. But if you burn me . . ."

"No burning. I swear on Beau."

Emery's face softened a bit. Swearing on our horses was sacred. "Just don't make me regret it, okay?"

"I won't. Thank you. If you want, you're welcome to come hang in my room while Vivi and I get out the whiteboard and try to figure this out."

Emery had no idea just how much I needed to solve this mystery. Beyond the hours and hours Vivi and I were sure to put into sleuthing, I had to look on my own, too.

"Thanks," Emery said. "I might take you up on that."

We smiled at each other. Shaky smiles, but still smiles. The anxiety knot in my stomach started to loosen. I'd been prepared for Emery to yell at me, tell me off, and say she never wanted to speak to me again. Even though she'd yelled, it had still gone better than I'd hoped. Now it was up to me—and Vivi—to figure out who had framed me.

"So, feel up to riding now?" I asked.

"Yeah. That sounds good."

Together, we turned back to the stable and headed for the entrance. Relief swept through my body as the adrenaline from the anxiety of the convo with Emery started to wear off. My limbs felt a bit limp now, and I took a deep breath. *I'll figure this out,* I thought.

"The stable is ridiculously gorgeous," Emery said slowly, tentatively. "Although you're probably used to it by now."

"Nope, definitely not." I shook my head. "I think that every time I see it."

"Bliss is down here," Emery said.

"Okay, I'm only a few stalls away, toward the end of the aisle."

"Want to grab our horses and meet in the middle?" Emery asked.

I nodded, and we headed for our horses' stalls. I reached Beau's and took his blue cotton lead rope from the hook outside his stall door.

"Hiya, handsome," I said, peering inside at him. Beau, who had been at his hay net, pricked up his ears and hurried over to me. "Hi, hi," I said, laughing. "Let me get the door open!" Beau took a polite step back, but the second I was inside, his muzzle pressed against my hands as he nosed me to say hello. "C'mon," I said, leading him out of his stall. "We're going on a ride with Bliss and Emery."

I halted him while I opened my tack trunk and grabbed his grooming kit. We joined Emery, who had her mesh-and-canvas grooming tote slung over her shoulder.

"Hi, Bliss," I said, smiling at the mare. She was a bright chestnut with a wide blaze and two socks. Bliss stretched out her neck to sniff Beau, and they huffed hellos to each other. We led them down to a side aisle with two pairs of free crossties, and it wasn't long before the horses were groomed and tacked up. Outside the stable, we put on our helmets and mounted.

"I've been thinking about what I could show you," I said. "I have an idea, if you're cool with a hack through the woods."

Emery nodded. "Sounds good to me."

"Let's go then," I said, squeezing my lower legs against Beau's sides.

As our horses made their way across the grass, I sneaked a look at Emery and was relieved to see that her eyes weren't shooting daggers at me. As long as I kept Emery—and everyone else—away from my real secret and unmasked the TXP, everything might be okay.

Hollow Rock Falls

WELL, I'M GLAD I MET YOU HERE after all," Emery said. "This is exactly what I needed." She loosened the reins a bit and let Bliss stretch her glossy neck as we walked our horses along a well-worn dirt path.

"Me too," I said. "But you haven't seen the best part yet. Trust me."

We were deep in the woods now. Thick trees surrounded us on both sides of the quiet marked trail. The air was still humid, but at least the sun was hidden behind puffy clouds. Plus, we had a lot of shade on the trails.

Emery looked over at me, and I felt her studying me. "You really didn't do it, did you?" she asked.

"No. I really didn't."

She blew out a breath. "Wow, yeah, I can see why you'd want to get away from everything and come out here."

"It sucks because we *just* got here—to the stable and to school. I was so excited all summer to get to Saddlehill and be back with my friends and classmates and riding buddies. Now? I just want to hide away in my room."

"You didn't do anything wrong," Emery said. "Someone did this to you. And to me. But mostly to you." She took a breath. "Now that I'm not so ragey, I can think past how it hurt me. You must feel violated."

I nodded. "And anxious. I don't know who did this or if I can trust anyone. Well, aside from Vivi and Thea."

"I'm sorry. That's an awful feeling. I mean, it's my first year here, and I know no one." She shook her head. "The last thing I want is an issue with someone."

"I highly doubt it's because of you. I must be some kind of magnet for people to try and mess with. There's a girl who's been giving me trouble since last year. She loves to make things hard for me whenever she can."

I held back from saying Selly's name, though. I didn't want Emery to think I was petty and biased against Selly just because of her position at the top of our equestrian team.

"So, do you think she did it?"

I shook my head. "I don't think so. I wish, because mystery solved! She's never been shy about getting directly in my face. So this underhanded approach isn't her style."

Emery nodded.

Plus, if Selly was going after me for what I'd done to her, there was no way she'd hide it from me. It would be an attack from all sides, and she would be very up-front about it.

The horses took a gentle right turn, and the thick cover of trees started to thin out as the mostly flat land turned a bit hilly, and we began going through a shallow ravine. Rocky cliffs jutted out to our right. The footing of the path changed from dirt to a mix of dirt and small gravel. We were getting close!

"I'm glad Vivi's going to help you figure this all out," Emery said. "Do you think you should tell an adult? Maybe your dad?"

I shook my head. "No, at least not yet. He'd just worry."

"True," Emery said, "but it's also kind of his job."

"I know, but I want to try and figure this out on my own first."

"Understandable. I'm sure you will." She gave me a sympathetic smile. I couldn't help but think about how all this progress past the TXP video would be ruined in an instant if Emery ever found out what I did to Selly. No way would she ever trust me again. Even thinking about it filled me with anxiety.

We rode in silence for a few minutes. The cliffs beside us grew taller and sharper. We wound our way down the ravine and came to a clear stream. It flowed fast but wasn't overpowering or scary.

"Is Bliss okay with water?" I asked. "I probably should have found that out before I brought you here."

"Oh, no worries," Emery said. "She loves water. Creeks, rivers, the beach—she doesn't care."

"Oh my god, you're so lucky! Beau is the biggest baby about water. Which is so ridiculous, since I try to take him to the horse-friendly part of the beach or the riverbank whenever I can." I gave an exaggerated sigh and patted his neck. "I'll keep him, but dang."

Emery laughed. "He *is* pretty cute!"

"It helps him get away with so much."

"Bliss, too," Emery said, shaking her head. "She's very puppylike when she wants something, with wide eyes and little grunts."

We laughed, and both of us leaned forward and patted our horses.

"Hear anything?" I asked.

Emery frowned. "No? Should I?"

I stayed quiet, letting her listen for a moment.

"Oh!" she said. "I hear something now! It sounds like a . . . I don't know! Giant air-conditioning unit? Small plane?"

"Not even close," I said. "But I like your guesses."

"Wha—" Emery started, then stopped. She saw it at the same time I did. Her mouth fell open a bit, and she blinked a bunch of times. "Are you kidding me?"

"Nope," I said, grinning. "Welcome to Hollow Rock Falls!"

We let the horses walk a few more yards before easing them to a halt near the waterfall. The main cascade fell from a rocky cliff at least forty feet high. Smaller cascades tumbled down from a few different levels of the cliff, and they all fell into a swimming hole below.

"Whoa," Emery said, "this is *breathtaking*."

"I know, right?" I leaned back in my saddle a bit as I tried to see the top of the falls. "We could have ridden around the perimeter of the stable, but you've already had a tour from Rebecca, so ehh. I wanted you to see this."

"It's one of the coolest things I've ever seen," Emery said. "Do you come out here a lot?"

"Not as much as I'd like. It takes a bit of time to get here, as you now know. I do like to come out in the winter at least once to see everything all iced over. The falls look like glass!"

Emery turned toward me, smiling. "We should come back once it's freezing then."

"Definitely. Right now, though, I'm hot," I said. "You?"

Emery nodded. "Very."

"Want to lose our socks and boots and stick our feet in the water?" I asked. "People usually bring bathing suits and hit the swimming hole under the falls. But since we've got the horses and no lead ropes to tie them, we'll have to make do with wading."

"That sounds awesome, as long as we keep our bare feet away from the horses' hooves," Emery said. "Let's do it."

We dismounted, tugged off our boots, and peeled off our

socks. We rolled up our breeches as much as the tight fabric would allow—which wasn't much—and walked into the shallow part of the stream that fed out from the deeper pool.

"This feels like heaven," I said, wiggling my toes in the water.

"It sure does."

Beau, hooves firmly planted in the dirt, stayed back far enough at the edge of the creek to keep his toes out of the water. "Beau S. St. Clair," I said, smiling at him. "C'mon. You can get your toes wet."

"Did I just hear you middle-initial your horse?" Emery asked.

"Yup, but he deserved it!"

"What does the S stand for?"

My cheeks warmed. "It's silly and it's not his registered name or anything, but 'Silver.' Like—"

"Sasha Silver," Emery said with a smile.

"I wanted to nickname him 'Beau Charm,' but that doesn't have the same ring to it."

"'Silver' is the perfect middle name for him."

I patted Beau's shoulder, then clucked at him, urging him forward.

"C'mon, Beau Silver St. Clair," Emery said. "Bliss is getting in!" Emery led her mare into the water, and Bliss stepped into the stream without hesitation.

Beau, ears flicking back and forth, watched Bliss lean down, sniff the water, and take a drink. "You got this," I told him. I moved my hand to hold the reins tighter under his chin and pulled. Beau finally took a tiny step. Then another. "There you go!" I said. "Good boy!" Beau took a few more timid steps until he was ankle-deep in the water.

"Yay, Beau!" Emery cheered. "Good job!"

Emery led Bliss closer to the falls, looking up at them. I stayed back with Beau and dug my toes into the bed of smooth rocks beneath my feet. I let go of Beau's reins, reached down into the water, and cupped some in my hands. I brought the water up to his forelegs before letting it run down back to the water. Taking my time, I repeated the process with each leg. I got his chest wet too, only stopping when he seemed to lose interest in what I was doing.

"We should come out here more," Emery called as she started making her way back over. "Maybe I could help you desensitize him?"

"That would be great," I said. "He needs it. He gets jumpy when we have to go through water during cross-country."

"I saw," Emery said. Then she raised a hand and smacked the front of her helmet. "I'm sorry! I didn't mean it like that!"

"No, it's okay. Everyone saw how we did at Fieldcrest. It was so, so bad."

"We all have those shows," Emery said. "It's a nightmare when it happens, but you've bounced back."

"We'll see if I have. I feel like I've grown since then, but I don't want to mess up like that ever, ever again."

"All we can do is cross our fingers," Emery said. "And practice, of course. But mostly cross our fingers."

I laughed. "You're so right." I fell quiet for a minute. "How is it that we never talked before that first dinner with our parents? I think we would have gotten along."

"I don't know, but I agree."

"That awkward, awkward dinner," I said, smiling despite myself. "Little did we know it would be the first of many."

"How my mom ever thought springing it on me that she was dating your dad was a good idea, I'll never know," Emery said.

"Same with my dad! He'd dated some before he'd met your mom, but nothing serious. Then, boom. Suddenly, it's all *very* serious and, oh, he's dating the mom of a rider I've never talked to before."

"Yup. My mom usually tells me everything. I'm pretty observant, too, so I don't know how I missed that she was getting serious about someone."

I reached forward with one hand and adjusted a section of Beau's mane that was sticking out. "I'm jealous of that," I said honestly. "My dad would do anything for me, but I feel like he doesn't know me that well. He works a ton, but still. Even when he was home, he was usually kind of absent."

Emery's eyes were on me, and she nodded. "I'm sorry. I didn't mean to make you feel bad when I talked about me and my mom."

"It's okay—you didn't. I just wish I had that with him. It's kind of impossible now that I'm away at school."

"Maybe he can FaceTime you more?" Emery suggested. "At first, when he and my mom set up Thursday evenings, I was like, how am I going to do that every week? But now I'm looking forward to it."

I frowned. "What's on Thursday evenings?"

"That's when the three of us will FaceTime every week," Emery explained.

"Oh."

I bit down hard on my lower lip so it wouldn't tremble as I

unfastened my helmet's chin strap. It felt like it was choking me. I didn't want Emery to know it bothered me. But my dad had a standing weekly FaceTime plan with her, and he didn't have one for me. That felt fantastic. Not. *Maybe you should feel good that he doesn't need a set date to FaceTime you, though,* I tried to tell myself. Dad could FT me anytime he wanted. But it didn't make me feel any better. In fact, it kind of bothered me more.

I fell quiet as Emery, seeming to know she'd said the wrong thing, started rambling about what we'd been talking about earlier: desensitizing Beau to water.

"I'm down to help," she said, her voice higher pitched than normal. "We can come out here again and next time, bring bathing suits."

"That would be cool," I said. I worked hard to keep any frustration out of my tone. It wasn't Emery's fault that my dad was paying attention to her. I knew that. But it didn't make it hurt any less. It also fed the flickers of insecurity deep inside that I was going to lose time with my dad to Emery.

"We can definitely help Beau. Right, Bl—" Emery stopped mid-sentence to shriek as her free arm windmilled and she slipped backward and landed with a giant splash on her butt in the water.

Before I could grab Beau's reins, he leaped sideways and skittered away from me.

"Easy!" I said, grasping at the reins that dangled around his neck. But I was too slow! My bare feet were slick against the stones, and I couldn't move fast enough to grab the reins. With a panicked snort, Beau charged out of the creek bed and up the gentle slope of the bank and tore off down the path.

Hide-and-Seek

I STOOD IMMOBILE IN THE CREEK BED, blinking. Beau had just bolted into the *woods*.

"Abby, oh my god, I'm so sorry!" Emery said, on her feet and hurrying over to me.

That snapped me out of my frozen state. "You didn't mean to. Are you okay?" Water soaked Emery's breeches and darkened the hem of her T-shirt.

Her cheeks were pink. "I'm totally fine. I slipped, and *of course* I had to splash and spook Beau."

"We need to find him," I said.

"You can ride with me on Bliss! We'll get him."

We hurried out of the creek bed and tugged our socks over our wet feet. I tried not to panic, but I was terrified.

"Omigod, Beau is the worst type of horse for this," I said, talking mostly to myself. "He's used to life in the pasture and in his stall." My panic level rose with every word. "He wouldn't know a poisonous plant from an edible one!"

Would he know how to follow the long path back to the stable, or would he go deeper into the woods and step on a thorn? Or get his reins caught on something? Or . . .

"Abby, don't," Emery said.

Wide-eyed, I glanced up at her. I hadn't even noticed she'd mounted. "What?" I asked.

"You're thinking the worst. I know he's not used to the woods, but we'll find him." Emery held out a hand to me. "Get on."

"You sure Bliss is okay with two riders?"

"Positive," Emery said.

I fastened my helmet's chin strap and mounted Bliss. It was kind of awkward for me to sit behind the saddle, but I wrapped my arms around Emery's waist. She nudged Bliss into a brisk walk.

Emery nodded. "You okay to trot?"

I squeezed her waist tighter. "Go for it."

Emery nudged Bliss into a trot. Bliss seemed to know we were looking for Beau. Her head was up high, and her ears swiveled as she looked from side to side. We wound our way down the path, keeping our eyes peeled for any sign that Beau had left the path and gone into the trees.

"What if we can't find him?" I wondered aloud. "What if he's lost deep in the woods?"

"He's smart, Abby," Emery said. "He probably headed for the stable, and someone saw he was loose and grabbed him."

Tears pricked my eyes. "I hope so. I'm really scared." Beau was my *everything*. If anything happened to him . . .

"We'll find him," Emery said, her voice firm. She nudged Bliss with her heels, and the mare moved into a faster trot.

With every passing minute, my panic level rose more and more. We were well away from the falls now, and there had been no sign of Beau. For a second, I wondered if I should call my dad. There wasn't anything he could do, exactly, but maybe I should call him. I didn't want to bother him, but—

"Stop, stop!" I said.

Emery pulled up Bliss. "What? Did you see something?"

I swung my leg over Bliss's rump and let myself slide to the ground. "I think I saw something move over there." I pointed into a patch of woods, squinting.

"I don't think you should go off the path," Emery said. "What if you get lost?"

"It could be Beau. I have to!"

"Okay, ugh, you're right. I'll stay here with Bliss. Do you have your phone?"

I patted it in the side pocket of my breeches. "Got it." Then I saw something move again. "Be right back!"

I took off at a jog, my eyes adjusting to the dim light as I crashed through a line of shrubs and headed for the place I'd seen movement. "Beau?" I called. "Beau? Come here, boy." A thorn snagged my T-shirt and my fingers stung when I freed myself, but I kept hurrying. I reached a clearing and stopped to look around me and listen. "Beau?" My voice wobbled as I tried not to cry.

Then I heard him. A whicker. Hooves thudding on dirt.

"Beau? Beau?" I kept saying his name over and over. I stayed where I was but turned toward the sound of his nicker. Beau, head down, emerged from a line of trees and overgrowth to the right of me. "Beau!" I jogged over to him, my arms out. The second I reached him, I flung my arms around his neck and squeezed him. "Omigod, Beau! Are you okay? I was so scared!"

I forced myself to let go of his neck, and while holding his reins, I bent over and ran my hands down his legs, feeling for any heat or nicks or scrapes. He seemed fine.

"Let's go get back on the trail," I said. "Bliss and Emery will be excited to see you."

It took us a bit longer to get back to the path since I'd dashed in solo, but now we had to find a way out that worked for both Beau and me. When I saw Emery waving, I almost sagged to the ground with relief.

"Omigod, you found him!" Emery cheered. "Yay!"

I led Beau back onto the path, and he craned his neck toward Bliss. They touched muzzles and let out matching contented huffs. I mounted and leaned forward in the saddle to hug Beau again.

"I'm going to be hugging him nonstop for a while," I said. "I'll probably have a total meltdown once we're out of the woods and back at the stable."

"I would too. He looks okay, thankfully!"

"He seems to be fine," I said. "I think this traumatized me more than it did him."

Emery laughed. "Probably! Ready to head back?"

"So ready. Let's go!"

"Next time, we bring a change of clothes, by the way," Emery said. "My legs and butt are going to be prunes after I take off these wet breeches."

I winced. "Agreed and same. So gross."

Together, we urged our horses into fast trots, leaving the woods behind. It was going to be a while before I came back after that scare.

XO, TXP

O N MONDAY MORNING, I HOPPED OUT of bed before my alarm went off. I was officially a seventh grader! I peered at myself in the mirror for a second. Nope, I didn't look magically older or more mature. Still the same round face with wide blue-green eyes. Maybe I'd look older after lunch.

Vivi groaned when her alarm started chirping.

"Morning!" I called to her.

"No" was her only response.

Laughing softly to myself, I checked my phone.

Dad had started a group text with Emery, Natalie, and me.

Hi, girls, he'd written. We love you, and happy first day!

The text made my head hurt. Part of me was glad he'd texted us. But the other part of me was sad. This wasn't a text to me. It was to *both* of us. So he had a standing weekly FaceTime with Emery and now group texts? I had to talk to him and say something. But I didn't know what. Or how.

With a sigh, I left the message on read and went over to check my email. I scrolled through, deleting the junk, and my eyes landed on the last new email's subject.

You're welcome!

Then I saw the sender.

Truth X. Poser

The words on the screen started to swim, and I felt like I couldn't breathe. I clicked on the message.

Hi, Blabby Abby!

How are you feeling? Much better I hope after the truth came out. Do you feel lighter? More at peace? I know I do! Ahhh, it felt so good to show your sister and all your friends just how insecure you really are. Hopefully, Little Sister got the message. If not, I'll have to try again. Oh, and Abby? Don't try to figure out who I am . . . or else. Who knows what secrets might be spilled next!

xo,

TXP

"Vivi?"

Vivi grunted in response. As I closed my email app, I thought for a moment, trying to calm my racing thoughts. This was my first day of school. Vivi's first day too, and if I told her about this now, it would ruin her day. She'd never get this first day of seventh grade back. Neither would I. *You are not going to have your day wrecked by a stupid email,* I told myself. There was so much good happening today—this year—and I wasn't going to let the "Truth X. Poser" ruin it for me.

Then Vivi sat up in bed and grinned at me. "It's the first day!" she cheered.

That smile on her face was the reason I had to keep the email a secret. At least for now. I could tell her tonight after classes. After I washed my face and brushed my teeth, I pulled on the outfit I'd spent hours and hours agonizing over: dark jeans, a fitted teal tee with teensy silver stripes, and a pair of white sneakers.

I swiped on lip gloss and a single coat of mascara. Once I had my messenger bag slung over my shoulder, I snapped a selfie and uploaded it to Instagram. *First day!* I captioned it, and posted the picture. It was officially time to kick off seventh grade, and I was going to have a good—no, a *great*—day!

After breakfast, I headed to my first class: art. I'd grown up taking basic art classes in school but hadn't developed an interest in it until late last year. I didn't have a lot of free time that didn't involve riding or studying horse care, but when I needed a break from the barn, I loved sketching. Mostly horses, flowers, and plants so far. But I wanted to expand what I was doing and get better at it, so this art class sounded like the perfect way to do that.

I snagged a desk in the middle of the classroom and pulled out my iPad and Apple Pencil and opened my notes app. It felt so comforting to be back in the classroom. I had always been an unapologetic nerd, and I loved school.

Soon the dozen other desks in the classroom were filled. I loved Saddlehill's small class sizes and all the individual attention I got. Plus, it made me feel grown-up that we had scheduling similar to *college*—no homeroom, just separate classes.

I glanced around at the other students, spotting Willa. She'd found a seat on the other side of the room, near the bay window. I wanted to go sit by her, but the desks on that side of the room were already full. Maybe next time, if we were allowed to switch seats.

A tall young woman walked into the classroom, shutting the door behind her. She rocked a cheery yellow blazer that popped against her dark skin, and she had a tiny pin of a bumblebee on her lapel.

"Good morning, everyone!" she said, giving us a big smile.

"Good morning," we all said back.

"I'm Sophia Foster, and welcome to seventh-grade art. Let's get attendance out of the way, and then we'll get started."

It didn't take Ms. Foster long to get all our names and

double-check our pronouns. She looked up from her tablet and put down her stylus.

"All right, class, let's begin," she said. "As I said, my name is Ms. Foster, and my pronouns are 'she' and 'her.' This is my first year teaching at Saddlehill. I want to make this an immersive learning environment that excites you and makes you hungry to learn everything about art."

I smiled, liking her already.

"This is an exploratory class to help foster—ha, get it?—your basic art skills," Ms. Foster continued. "I hope all of you signed up for this class because you wanted to, not because you had to."

I nodded. Definitely.

Ms. Foster said, "This class meets Mondays and Wednesdays. If you look at your schedule, however, you will see occasional Fridays, too. That means if we have a big class project and need more time, I'll schedule a Friday period to work with you and check on your progress. Make sense?"

Again, I nodded. I loved the two-days-a-week schedule, but it was comforting to have the occasional Fridays too, in case we didn't get everything done.

"Let's all pull up the syllabus on our tablets, and you

can follow along with me while I go over a few things," Ms. Foster said.

She gave us a minute to find ours, then dove right in.

"As I was saying, this is an exploratory class designed to improve your basic art skills. If you're a more advanced artist, this class would be a great refresher for areas of yours that may need some attention," she said. "We're going to cover drawing, painting, sculpting, and artwork design."

I smiled when she said "sculpting." That was something I'd never done before! I couldn't wait to try, though.

"We'll work on developing your artistic eye and your creativity," Ms. Foster said. "With each unit, we'll learn about the art elements from shapes, colors, values, forms, texture, and lines. We'll also get into the design principles."

I highlighted those things on my syllabus. It sounded like everything in this class would help me with my artwork.

"Don't get overwhelmed," Ms. Foster said. "I know, I know, this sounds like a lot. But we have all year to work through these topics. In my class, you'll be graded on quizzes, your class participation, and how much effort you put into your work." She cleared her throat. "If anyone signed up for this class because you thought it would be an easy A, please do yourself a favor and go see your guidance counselor about withdrawing."

That made me gulp, even though it wasn't directed at me. But I'd be annoyed if I were a teacher and students only took my class because they didn't expect to have to try.

"There will also be group art projects and individual projects," Ms. Foster said. "Our first big project will be creating abstract art to present to the class."

That made me sit up straighter. Group art projects sounded like so much fun!

"So, let's begin our first discussion," Ms. Foster said. "Before I pull up some examples to show you, I want to hear from you all first. What do you think of when you hear 'abstract art'?"

Hmm. I settled back in my seat.

"It doesn't need to be a textbook definition," Ms. Foster said. "Just whatever you think of."

Willa raised her hand. "Odd shapes and lots of colors."

Ms. Foster nodded. "Great! Who else?"

A guy next to me, I think his name was Zayn, raised his hand. "I think of art that's not always on a canvas. It could be a wall with fake petals glued to it."

"That's excellent, Zayn," Ms. Foster said.

A couple of other students raised their hands before I put mine up. Ms. Foster nodded at me.

"I think of 3D art," I said. "And art that doesn't have to always have precise lines or shapes."

Ms. Foster smiled. "Wonderful. Thank you all for sharing. I love hearing your thoughts before getting into a lecture. That's how I plan to structure this class, by the way. There is always going to be room for discussions and hearing about what art makes you think and feel."

As Ms. Foster got into the lecture and I started taking notes, all I could think about was how excited I was to take this class. This day—minus the Truth X. Poser, of course—was off to a great start, and I crossed my fingers on my left hand that it would continue.

Forever a Horse Girl

THE REST OF THE SCHOOL DAY WAS A
flurry of classes, meeting new teachers, and finding
my way to each classroom.

After classes, I changed and grabbed the bus to the stable.
Rebecca had texted and asked me to swing by her office before
our lesson. Sweat already prickled along my lower back, and
my feet were sweaty in my boots. I'd only been outside for a
few minutes too. So. Gross.

The stable grounds buzzed with activity. The outdoor
pens were all occupied as riders exercised their horses on

lunge lines, which were like long lead ropes that allowed the horse to circle the rider while they cued the horse from the ground. One of the lower-level instructors, Allie, was in one of the big outdoor arenas, setting up some ground poles for exercises.

I crossed my fingers that all the outdoor arenas were spoken for, because that meant we could wind up in the covered indoor arena with the pitched roof. It was my absolute favorite during the summer, because we had protection from the too-hot sun but got a great cross breeze.

As I walked into the barn, I inhaled the most comforting scent in the world: horses. The smell was a straight shot of serotonin into my brain. The mix of scents of sweet grains, fresh hay, and clean sawdust made me feel comforted. There was nothing better.

Rebecca's office door was open, so I peered inside. She was at her desk, staring intently at her laptop screen.

"Hey, hope I'm not bothering you right now," I said, knocking lightly on the doorjamb.

Rebecca looked up, blinking. "Oh, no, not at all!" She closed her laptop lid. "Come on in and have a seat."

I slid into the plush leather office chair across from her

and tried not to crack my knuckles. It was a nervous habit I'd picked up.

"It's so nice to see you one-on-one," Rebecca said. "I wanted to have some face time and see how you're doing."

Whew. I relaxed into the chair. I'd had no idea what this was going to be about, but it wasn't bad at all.

"I'm good!" I said. "Glad to be back. It's nice to chat with you, too. It's hard to talk during lessons."

Rebecca nodded. "For sure. I want to meet with all my riders individually, and I knew you'd be here early grooming Beau before our lesson, so I thought I'd bring you in."

"I try not to skip any days with him if I can help it. I miss him too much."

My instructor smiled. "I know that feeling. Are you ready for show season to start this weekend?"

"So, sooo ready!" I said, excitement creeping into my voice. "I have a lot to prove after last year."

Rebecca shook her head. "No, you don't, Abby."

"Yes, I do. I bombed at the classic and didn't do great at regionals." I was quiet for a moment. "I let everyone down, including myself."

"Hey." Rebecca leaned forward in her desk chair, her

warm brown eyes locking on mine. "First, you didn't 'bomb' anything. You were off, and you panicked. It happens to everyone. Second, you didn't let any of us down. I'm sorry you let yourself down, though, because not for one second was I upset or mad or anything but proud of you."

"Thank you. I know we talked about it right after, but I've also had all summer to obsess over it, and the more I thought about it, the more embarrassed I got. I want to *crush* regionals this year. Crush. Them."

"I like your attitude," Rebecca said, smiling. "Let's focus on one thing at a time. For now, anyway. And for you, that's this weekend's show."

I nodded. "I'm ready. Whatever it takes, I'm going to do it."

"I want you to do what makes you proud of yourself," Rebecca said, "and not what you think will make others proud of you. I guarantee you, we already are."

My cheeks felt warm as I dipped my head, hiding a smile. "Thank you."

"You're welcome. Now, there's one thing I need from you."

"Anything," I said. I meant it too. I would do whatever Rebecca needed.

Rebecca leaned back in her chair, folding her hands on

top of her desk. "Excellent. I would like you to keep an eye on Emery."

I blew out a small breath. "Oh."

"As you know, I worked with her on and off this summer for her evaluation," Rebecca said. "Her talent is outstanding. I was blown away."

I nodded. "She's good."

"I want to make sure she handles adjusting to school and life away from home plus the riding team," Rebecca said. "So I would love it if you became her stable buddy of sorts. Make sure she's got someone to hang out with and talk to when you're tacking up and grooming the horses. Take her on a beach trip before it gets cold. Go on a hack. Trail ride! If you can't take her, find a friend who can. Help her meet other riders on the team."

"I introduced her to Zoe and Wren," I said. "She seemed to get along with them."

"That's great! But I still want you involved and spending time with her too, okay?"

"Of course."

The thought of spending more time with Emery made me sort of anxious. Sure, we'd patched things up after the video, but what if she wasn't as good as she'd said? Hanging out could get awkward. Fast.

"I know you're busy and have your own friends," Rebecca said, "but think back to how you felt last year. Brand-new school. Brand-new stable. New everything. It can be overwhelming. I wish I'd thought sooner to pair up new riders with vets."

I softened a bit. Last year *had* been tough. I hadn't known a single person. Beau was the only one I knew, and I'd spent so much time wishing for a friend. Then I'd met Thea. And later, Vivi. But being alone at school and the stable had been hard and lonely.

"I do remember what it feels like to be new," I said softly. "If I can help Emery adjust, I will. Promise."

"Thank you." Rebecca smiled. "I knew I could count on you."

With that, I left Rebecca's office and headed to groom Beau. I walked down the aisle, and when I got to Beau's stall, I peered around the black iron bars and laughed to myself at what I saw.

Bits of hay clung to Beau's mane and forelock. He had one eye semi-closed, blinking slowly with the other as if I'd just woken him up from a deep nap. A deep nap where he'd lost a fight with his hay net.

"Rough night, boy?" I asked him.

Beau blinked, his long black eyelashes fluttering, and stepped toward the front of his stall. Even after owning him for two years, I'd yet to get over how handsome he was.

"I'm feeling soft," I said as I opened his stall door and eased inside. "It's our anniversary next week." I threw my arms around him, hugging him tight. Beau let me cling to him and didn't move. "Are you sick of me yet? You can tell me." I let go of his neck and reached outside his stall for a lead rope. "Maybe you want to go live with someone else? Someone who will let you spend all your days napping in the pasture?"

I swear, Beau stared me down for a solid five seconds with a dirty look. As dirty as he could.

"All right, all right!" I said, laughing. "Too bad. Even if you wanted to go, I'm never letting you. You're my number one guy." I couldn't imagine my life without him. He'd helped me learn how to be happy again after my mom left. I leaned on him, trusted him, and counted on him.

I led him out of the stall and clipped him into crossties. Then I reached into my tack trunk and grabbed his grooming tote. Dad had gotten me a new black tote with gold stitching—the colors of our riding team—last year. After I closed the lid of my trunk, I put the tote on top and grabbed the hoof pick. It didn't take long for me to clean the dirt away from Beau's hooves.

"Since I'm all up in my feels today," I said to him, "do you remember the first time I groomed you after we brought you home?"

Beau blinked. I took it as a sign that yes, he did remember.

"You were so good," I told him. "Even though you were in a strange new place at Bayview, you fell asleep when I got out the brushes."

I could see the moment so clearly, it was almost as if it were playing out in front of me all over again. Beau had cocked a back hoof, and with one last twitch of his tail, he'd fallen into a deep sleep. I kept right on grooming him, running my hands along his back and shoulders and giving him gentle pats and massages while he snoozed. I remembered feeling honored that Beau had fallen asleep so easily on his first day with me. I'd been so lucky to find him and to get him as my first horse.

I'd grown up on fuzzy ponies at Bayview, but after I started riding for the Interscholastic Pony League, Dad thought it was time for me to have a horse of my own. A permanent mount that I wouldn't have to share with anyone. My dad and I had many, many talks about it, and after I promised to care for the horse as much as possible, he put out the word to the area horse community, and so did Chris, my then instructor.

By a twist of fate, a girl who rode at a nearby stable was heading to college soon and wasn't able to take her horse. She'd been competing on him with the IPL for a couple of years, and while he was still a bit green in some areas as a then five-year-old, he was also a sweetheart and eager to please.

I went to her stable and met Beau. It was the clichéd love at first sight. After I rode him and hung out with him for a bit, Dad and I headed home. During the car ride, Dad called Bayview's vet and asked her to go check out Beau. Dad knew it just like I did—Beau was the one for me.

"Two years together," I said to Beau. "Wow."

Grabbing a curry comb, I started working on Beau's back and rump. As I groomed him, more riders came to the barn and began prepping to ride. The mood felt light and cheery, as we were all excited to be back. But as I looked at each of them, I couldn't help but wonder: Was the Truth X. Poser among us? Was the person who set me up here right now?

Taking a deep breath, I tried to relax. But I was worried about riding with Selly and Nina today, sure they would have something snide to say about the video. Keir wouldn't. He'd done the sweetest thing ever and texted me this morning to say I had no reason to be weird at practice. He believed me, and he hoped I caught the TXP. But where Keir was kind and looking out for me, I knew Selly and Nina would surely have something biting to say. I had to put on my armor and be ready to fend off their attacks.

Toxic

I T DIDN'T TAKE ME TOO LONG TO GET BEAU'S coat gleaming. The stable had quieted down a bit as riders tacked up their own mounts and headed out to ride.

Beau stood quietly—the perfect gentleman—while I smoothed a quilted navy saddle pad onto his back. Once it was positioned just right, I swiped my saddle off my tack trunk and lifted it onto Beau's back. Thankfully, he was as easy to tack up as he was to groom. After I tightened the girth, I got him buckled into his bridle with a gentle snaffle bit.

"Ready to go, boy?" I asked him.

He lifted his head high and blinked his deep brown eyes as I grabbed my crop and put on my black helmet. I owed it to Beau to focus on the lesson at hand and not ruin it by getting distracted thinking about the TXP.

"Let's do it!" I told him.

Together, we headed down the aisle. I peered through the window of the indoor arena and saw Nina, Emery, and Selly warming up their horses inside. My heart raced as I spotted a beautiful jump course. I hoped that was for us!

One thing I hadn't missed all summer? Riding with Selly. Sharing a space with her was the opposite of fun. Selly had been comfortable at the top of our team last year, but her reign was over. I wanted that number one team spot this year and all that came with it.

Emery spotted us and walked Bliss over. "Hey," she said, and brought Bliss to a halt in front of us.

"It looks like I got the right arena," I said. As the words came out of my mouth, I cringed. It made me think about— *no*. No, now was *not* the time to think about that.

"Yup," Emery said. "Rebecca texted everyone to meet here instead of outside."

I shook my head. "Oh, I didn't see it."

"Whoops," Emery said. "At least you found us."

I checked Beau's girth, then swung myself into the saddle. Once I was settled, I squeezed my legs against his sides and let him stretch his neck as we ambled beside Bliss and Emery. As I stared between Beau's pricked ears, I rolled my shoulders and tried to let the tension seep away.

"How excited are you?" I asked Emery, thinking of Rebecca's request. "Your first lesson with the team."

"I'm excited with a heavy side of nervous," she said. "It's scary riding with the team for the first time."

I glanced over at Emery, giving her a sympathetic smile. "I'm sorry you're nervous. Try to remember that Rebecca wouldn't have let you join our group if she didn't think you could handle it. Plus, I've seen you ride. You're going to do fine."

Emery gave me a small smile. "Thanks, Abby. That helps a lot, honestly."

Still, I saw her hand shake as she smoothed Bliss's mane. We let the horses walk down the side of the arena on loose reins.

Selly angled her dark bay mare, Ember, beside Beau, and Nina let her gray gelding, Adore, walk on Emery and Bliss's right side.

"Hey, Em!" Selly chirped, smiling at her. "The river party

was so hectic, but I'm glad we got to talk that night. It was great to get to know you better."

Huh? I looked from Selly to Emery and then back to Selly. When had those two talked? I shook my head. I'd missed their interaction at the river. And since when did she call Emery "Em"?

"Thank you!" Emery said, a smile spreading across her face. "It was nice to talk to you, too."

"How are you feeling?" Selly asked Emery. Her tone was a bit somber now. "Anything you need, feel free to ask me. Not to hype myself up, but I'm the biggest cheerleader on this team, and I want you to fit right in."

I could not believe what I was hearing. Selly, the biggest cheerleader? Being . . . *nice?*

"I'm nervous," Emery said, "but also ready to go." She learned forward, patting Bliss's glossy shoulder. "Bliss seems to like it here!"

The mare did look relaxed in the arena—her tail swishing gently as she walked and one ear pointed forward and one back to listen for possible verbal cues from Emery.

Selly waved a hand. "Oh, please, you have nothing to worry about. I've seen you compete. You're *so* good. We can all learn from you."

Um, what? I frowned. Selly didn't hand out compliments about riding. Or anything. *Ever.* The last thing she would want was Emery to swoop in here and become the new team star. I didn't know what her game was, but she was *so* up to something.

"Wow," Emery said. "That's really, really kind of you, thanks! But I'm going to be learning from everyone, including you, Selly."

Selly grinned. "I think you're going to fit in just fine on this team."

The words coming out of Selly Hollis's mouth did not match the girl I'd gotten to know last year. At all!

"And how are you, Abby?" Selly asked.

"Good?" I said. She never asked how I was, so I couldn't help but respond in a questioning tone.

"I'm glad you and Emery are okay after, well," Selly said, stage-whispering, "after that video."

"It was a fake," I said quickly. "I'm going to find out who did it."

Selly laughed, then gave me a patronizing smile. "I'm sure you will."

I squeezed my legs against Beau's sides and asked him to move into a trot just so I could get some space for a moment. I needed to forget about Selly and focus on my ride. Worrying about Selly was not on my list of steps to win this year.

I posted to Beau's trot, waving at Thea and Keir, who had entered the arena on their horses and were starting to warm up too.

This was it. This was my group for the year.

Keir.

Selly.

Nina.

Emery.

Thea.

And me.

Sure, some of the other older, more experienced riders like Maia would join us from time to time so we could ride with them, but my core group was here.

As I turned Beau and rounded the corner at the other end of the arena, I looked at Selly, Nina, and Emery. Their horses walked side by side, and the girls laughed at something Nina said as she gestured while she spoke. Anxiety made my stomach flip-flop. I didn't want to tell Emery who to be friends with, and I didn't want her to think I didn't like Selly because of petty reasons. But the girl was toxic, and the last thing I wanted her to do was poison Emery.

Before I could dwell on it, Rebecca strode into the arena, a smile on her face and a neon-blue clipboard in her hand.

"Good afternoon, riders!" she called, waving an arm. "C'mon over and line up in front of me."

I took a deep breath and guided Beau over to a spot in front of my coach. Keir halted his chestnut gelding, Magic, next to me. Emery was on my other side with Thea, and the rest of my teammates lined up from there.

"I'm so glad to see all of you today," Rebecca said. "First of all, let's give an official welcome to Emery Flynn. This is her first year riding with us."

Emery raised her hand and waved. "Hey!"

"I worked with Emery over the summer," Rebecca continued, "and I got to see firsthand what kind of rider she was and what strengths she will bring to our team. Not only will she be on the stable's IPL team, but she will join this group for lessons and competitions. She is a talented young rider who will bring so much to our team."

I didn't have to look at Emery to know she was blushing. I would be. Compliments from Rebecca meant the most because she didn't give them out freely, and when she complimented you, she meant every word.

Rebecca looked at Emery and smiled. "Emery, welcome to our team! I'm so excited to have you, and I hope you're ready to learn and grow with us."

"Thank you," Emery said softly. "I am. I'm ready."

Rebecca clapped, and the rest of us joined in.

"Have you met all the riders here?" Rebecca asked her.

Emery nodded. "Yup, I've talked to everyone."

"Great," Rebecca said. "You'll get to know them all even more as we dig into the show season. If you have questions about anything, please let me know. Or talk to one of your fellow riders, okay?"

"Like me," Selly sweetly offered. "I'm always here to help a teammate."

I held back a snort.

"I will," Emery said. "Thank you!"

"Good," Rebecca said. "We're going to need everyone at the top of their game to get to nationals this year."

"And beat Canterwood Crest," Selly said. "That's my biggest goal."

"Mine, too!" Thea chimed in.

"Saaame," I said. I rolled my eyes just thinking of the Connecticut boarding school's top-tier riders.

"I'm over them always being at the top," Keir said. "Every. Single. Year."

"Don't they have enough blue ribbons by now?" Nina joked.

Rebecca laughed, nodding. "They got our nationals team last year," she said. "But not by much. Let's hope we make it all the way again so you can face off against them."

"So we can *win* against them!" I said.

My teammates cheered.

Long before nationals, we'd *definitely* see them at area and regional competitions. But I was ready.

This year was going to be different.

It was *our* turn.

It was *my* turn. I wasn't going to mess up this time.

"In order to put us in the best possible position for success," Rebecca said, "there are going to be some changes to the team structure. Now that we have Emery, we're going to break into two teams of three."

Oh my god. I mean, I'd suspected that since we had another person. But *yikes*, what if I ended up on a team with Selly and Nina? I shot Thea a grimace, and she was wide-eyed when she looked over at me.

"Also, I'm going to designate a captain for each team. This person will be a representative of sorts for their team."

I watched Selly sit up straight, grinning at Rebecca. This was our first year with a shot at being team captains. Last year, it had been an older rider who had moved on to a different division this year.

"The captains will be in place for half the show season," Rebecca said. "Then we'll switch it up, or if those people are doing an outstanding job, they will remain as captains. I've taken a lot into account, from your performances last year to how helpful you have been toward fellow riders to how much I can depend on you to be there for the team."

I crossed my fingers. I doubted it would be me this year, but I couldn't help but have a little bit of hope.

"So, teams," Rebecca said. "Our first team will be Thea, Abby, and Nina."

Inside, I broke out into a happy dance. No Selly on my team! I grinned, looking over at Thea. She gave me a thumbs-up, her smile as big as mine.

"Thea, you're team captain," Rebecca said, nodding at her.

"Yesss!" Thea said, letting out a victory whoop.

"Yaaay!" I cheered, clapping. Thea would be a great captain! She'd had a stellar season last year, so it made sense that Rebecca had chosen her to lead our team. I was so happy for her, and it made me determined to prove to Rebecca that I deserved to be team captain next. Beau and I could work harder than ever between now and the midpoint of the show season.

"That means team two is Selly, Emery, and Keir," Rebecca said. "Keir, congratulations! You'll be team two's captain."

Everyone clapped, and Keir grinned.

The only person not clapping? Selly.

"How is Keir our team captain?" Selly blurted out. An angry flush crept up her neck to her cheeks. "I had a better season last year!"

Rebecca folded her arms. "Selly, don't be a poor sport."

"I'm not! I just—I don't understand," Selly said.

"Selly, you know team captains aren't chosen simply on their show record," Rebecca said. "I consider how much you put into practices, how well you work with others, and how responsible you are. Plus, we've talked about your attitude before, and what you said just now isn't helping your case."

Selly pressed her lips together for a second. "Okay,

sorry. I'm upset, but it's only because I love this team so much! I'll do better, Rebecca. You can count on me."

"Unfortunately, you were late to one of your classes at a show last year, resulting in missing your start time and being disqualified. That's a big, big deal."

Oh god. My stomach dropped.

"That wasn't my fault!" Selly protested. "I didn't—"

"Selly," Rebecca said, a warning in her tone. "I thought by now you'd take responsibility for yourself in that situation. We've discussed this. You're the one in charge of making sure you get to practices and classes on time."

Rebecca was right about personal responsibility. Except in this case, Selly's lateness and missing her start time hadn't been her fault.

It had been *mine*.

Last year, an entire group of competitors had dropped out due to food poisoning from bad takeout, and the show officials had moved our show-jumping start times earlier and had posted the new time on the whiteboard inside the tack room. The message had been there for hours, so I'd assumed everyone had seen it when I'd erased it to write up a question for the grooms about the feed schedules.

After I'd written my question and left the tack room, I'd gotten nervous that maybe everyone *hadn't* seen it. So, minutes later, I'd gone back, erased my message, and rewritten the note.

We'd started the day's competition, and when it was Selly's turn, she was nowhere to be found. She showed up after her start time, and even after arguing with the officials and Rebecca, she'd been out. Disqualified. She got a lecture from Rebecca about checking the whiteboard. Selly had insisted she had, and that the time was posted as ten a.m. Rebecca said she was a thousand percent sure she'd read the adjusted time, and it was clear it had been posted correctly, since everyone had made it except Selly. And when Selly took Rebecca to the tack room to show her, the board had been wiped. Probably by an innocent groom, but no one knew for sure.

And while my face had burned in shame, I'd sat in Beau's saddle and realized what I'd done. That I had messed up and written the old time instead of the new one, causing Selly to be late, miss her class, and get disqualified. Selly had fumed, and rightfully so. She'd competed in an extra show a few weeks later to try and get her season points back up, but that

DQ had hurt her, and she hadn't been able to have the perfect season she'd been on track to have.

Now I'd cost Selly her shot at team captain this time around too.

Let's See How Good
You Are ... or Aren't

I TRIED TO SHAKE AWAY THE GUILT FROM the awful memory. There was nothing I could do about it. Telling Selly the truth now would only make her come after me. She would *destroy* me if she ever found out. Once I'd realized what I'd done, I'd tried to covertly make it up to Selly, but her not making team captain because of my mistake—I didn't know how I'd ever make it up to her for that.

Selly gritted her teeth together and took a deep breath. "Congratulations, Keir." She set her jaw.

There wasn't an ounce of happiness for him in her tone.

"Your excitement is overwhelming," he said, sounding only half-joking.

Rebecca cleared her throat. "After the lesson, if you want to speak in private, Selly, we can do that. But I highly advise that you support Keir in his role as captain and work toward proving yourself."

Selly nodded, her chin still jutted out and her back ramrod straight. What had I done? She was going to give everything she had for team captain next time. It was going to make my job a hundred times harder to get one of the two spots. But I wasn't going to give up without a fight.

"Moving on," Rebecca said. "I don't want you to think showing is our only focus, because to help us win *and* be better-rounded equestrians, we will have unmounted meetings too. Our unmounted meetings will focus on learning more about our equine friends, from their health and well-being to how to care for them properly to traveling safely and any other topics I deem important."

Keir raised his hand, and Rebecca nodded at him.

"Are we going to have a quiz rally this year?" he asked.

Rebecca smiled. "I'm so glad you asked! Yes, we are. We're going to have one later this fall for some fun prizes. We'll be going head-to-head with other area stables, so it's going to be quite a big competition. We'll talk about it more later, but we'll have plenty of time to learn, study, and prepare."

I looked over at Emery, and she caught my eye, trading a smile with me.

"Our first show is this weekend, so it's game time," Rebecca said. "Everyone's warmed up, right?"

Each of us nodded.

"Excellent," Rebecca said. "So, the plan for today is simple: this course isn't focused on height—it's about your ride. I want to see how well you and your horse handle it. You'll each take the course, one at a time, and after each rider goes, we'll all give that person constructive feedback. Got it?"

"Yes," I said along with everyone else.

I wanted a clean ride. A ride so clean it would be hard for anyone to find something to pick on.

Rebecca looked at her clipboard, then back up at us. "Let's see where you are after summer break."

I shot a glance at Thea, and we were both all smiles. It felt so good be back in training. My entire group—minus Emery—hadn't worked with Rebecca all summer because we'd been at our home stables. Most of us had taken some lessons from our instructors there, but we'd mainly worked solo. And that was nothing like lessons with Rebecca.

"First, you'll pop over that single cross rail," Rebecca said. "Then you'll ride toward the end of the area before taking the second cross rail."

As Rebecca talked, my eyes followed along on the course.

"You'll make a bending line and take the first oxer, make a half circle, jump the blue-and-white vertical, and then do a rollback before the fifth jump—another vertical. Then come around, and you'll hit the outside line with the vertical and final jump—the oxer."

I was ready. I wanted to go, go, go!

"Any questions?" Rebecca asked.

No one raised their hands.

"Let's have Thea go first," Rebecca said. "Chaos looks extra ready to go right now." She walked over to him, patting his shoulder.

"Thank you," Thea said with a sheepish smile. "He's full of energy today! What else is new, right?"

Chaos's coat had started to darken with sweat. He struck the dirt with a foreleg—impatient and ready for Thea to let him move. But she held firm and kept him standing in line until he quieted a bit.

"Everyone else, move your horses out of the way," Rebecca directed us. "Thea, you may start whenever you're ready."

I gave my bestie a thumbs-up and squeezed my legs against Beau's sides. We joined Emery, Keir, Selly, and Nina out of Chaos's path.

Thea rolled her shoulders back, straightened a bit, and let Chaos into a fast trot before sitting deep in the saddle and asking him to canter. Despite Chaos's energy, he still paid attention to Thea and had an active canter that collected and lengthened when she asked. It was hard not to be awed when I watched him. He could be a handful, however, and lived up to his name sometimes. But Thea was a super-calm rider and knew just when to hold him back and when to let him go. She was one of my favorite riders to watch.

Chaos, ears pricked forward, cantered toward the cross rail and leaped over it without incident. He jumped higher than nec-essary, though. If it had been a longer, more demanding course, he would burn through so much energy. Thea managed to hold him steady over the next few jumps, and when they cleared the final oxer, I dropped my reins against Beau's neck and clapped.

"Nice, Thea!" I cheered.

She was all smiles when she trotted Chaos over to us.

"I'll hold my comments until everyone has offered their critiques," Rebecca said. It was impossible not to see the smile she was hiding, though. "Let's start with Nina and go down the line."

"That was a good ride," Nina said. "You made it seem pretty effortless, even though I've ridden Chaos before, and I know he can be a lot of work."

"Thanks!" Thea said, patting his neck.

Keir said almost the same as Nina, and then it was Selly's turn.

"I'm not going to lie or anything," Selly said. "Unlike those two."

Sigh. Why was she like this?

"Selly," Rebecca warned. "Make sure that what you're about to say is constructive."

Selly shot Rebecca a megawatt smile. "Oh, it is! Of course."

I shook my head ever so slightly. To her credit, Thea pressed her lips together into a tight line and didn't attempt to talk back to Selly.

"I'm sure you know what I'm going to say," Selly said. "It's obvious. Chaos was so excitable that he jumped much higher than necessary on many of the jumps. He wasted tons of energy. And if he doesn't get in better shape, he'll be beat after a relatively low degree of difficulty course."

Okay, I wouldn't have delivered it that way, but Selly had said what I'd been thinking.

Thea nodded, bowing her head for a second. "Thanks, Selly. I agree."

Still, I bristled a bit for my best friend. Selly didn't have to say everything with such an attitude, did she? Thankfully, Thea got constructive feedback from Emery, Rebecca, and me—I echoed Selly's thoughts about Chaos's jumping height while still being kind.

"Emery," Rebecca said. "Please go next."

With a small smile, Emery urged Bliss away from the rest of the horses and toward the start. My own heart rate sped up as I waited, watching her circle Bliss and prepare to take the course.

Crush It or
Crushed by It?

EMERY TROTTED BLISS IN A HALF CIRCLE before letting the mare into a slow, easy canter.

"She's going to crush it," Selly said to Nina. But she was loud enough so I could hear. I still didn't know why Selly was so invested in Emery, but I had a feeling it was solely because she thought it would rattle me.

Emery and Bliss headed for the first cross rail, taking it with no problem. Bliss was quiet under Emery as they made a sweeping half turn and popped gracefully over the oxer and headed for the vertical.

I shook my head as I watched. Wow. Just wow. Once my dad had told me he was dating Emery's mom, I'd watched some of her shows to see what she was like in the arena. She'd been good then, but the lessons from Rebecca earlier this summer had clearly paid off. Emery rode with such confidence, and Bliss was in tune with her every movement. It was beautiful to watch.

Bliss snapped her legs under her, taking the oxer with glee. As they cantered around the rest of the course, they moved in sync to tackle each jump.

She's better than you, I thought. *There's no way your ride will look that good.* Ugh. *Stop,* I told my brain. This wasn't a competition. *Yet.* This was practice.

"Told you," Selly said to Nina. "She's so much better than Abby. I'm glad Abby's not on my team."

I whipped my head in their direction, ready to say something. Anything! But I didn't want Rebecca to notice us talking. We were going to get in trouble if we didn't pay attention to Emery's ride, and I didn't want to be assigned mucking duty.

Bliss jumped the last obstacle with ease—clearing the oxer with zero hesitation. Emery rode her in a half circle before turning back to face us. A grin stretched from ear to ear, and she leaned down to pat Bliss's shoulder.

"Nice job," I said, clapping. I wasn't going to let Selly know I'd heard her. Or let her think I was worried about Emery. Nope. Not for a second. Plus, good sportsmanship was something that had been instilled in me since my first riding lesson. I wasn't going to not cheer on a fellow rider. The rest of my teammates clapped too.

"Thanks!" Emery said to all of us as she halted Bliss. The mare tossed her head, her forelock flying as she snorted. She was proud too. She knew how well their ride had gone.

"Thea, start us off," Rebecca said.

Thea blew out a breath. "We're supposed to look for problems with the ride, but wow, Emery. I'm having a hard time here." Thea laughed. "I guess if anything, I'd say to watch your balance, but that's it. That was a great ride!"

Emery blushed. "Thank you!"

"Abby?" Rebecca asked, nodding at me.

I trained my gaze on Emery, and she gave me a small smile. She looked nervous all over again. Like she was afraid I was going to rip her ride apart.

"That was a really nice ride," I said. "I agree with Thea—I

think you leaned on your hands a couple of times. So you need some core work. Other than that, you should be really proud."

Emery smiled, looking down, then back up at me. "Thank you," she said softly. "I really appreciate that!"

"Selly, go ahead," Rebecca said.

"I'm *so* glad you're on my team! Oh my gosh, that ride was everything! I'm going to agree with Abby and Thea on the hands issue, but otherwise, that was a gorgeous ride."

I squinted, looking over at Selly. *Gorgeous?* When did Selly ever call someone's ride "gorgeous"? Also, gushing over someone wasn't Selly. She didn't gush over Nina's rides. Ever.

"Wow, thanks!" Emery said.

Selly smiled at her, then glanced over at me. She smirked before looking back at Rebecca.

Nina and Keir reiterated what Thea, Selly, and I had said with glowing praise. No one could find much to pick on.

"I agree with your teammates," Rebecca said. "For a first course after summer break, you were so clean. I want to work on your seat when we get into hard-core flatwork, though. There were a few unnecessary bounces in there, and you opened your hip angle instead of folding back a couple of times. But a great ride and an excellent way to start your time with us, so thank you."

Emery beamed. I couldn't help but feel a small rush of pride.

Selly rode next, and her ride was just as great as Emery's. She had the perfect blend of Thea's quiet, calm vibes mixed with Emery's confidence.

When it was my turn to give a critique, I took a deep breath. "That was a great ride. Ember got tight toward the end, but I think you worked through that well. Your reins were a bit long in places, though, so maybe keep that in mind."

Selly stared at me, and I could see her calculating whether she could snap back at me or if she'd pushed her luck already today with Rebecca.

"Thanks" was all she said.

As I listened to the rest of Selly's good feedback, my stomach dropped. I was going to have to work extra hard to look good next to them, but I was 100 percent up for the challenge.

After we finished critiquing Selly, Rebecca nodded at me. "You're up, Abby," she said.

"Okay," I said, squeezing my legs against Beau's sides. Once I was away from my teammates, I took a long, deep breath. *It's an easy course,* I told myself. *Trust Beau, and he won't steer you wrong.* But anxiety churned in my stomach. What if *I* steered *him* wrong?

Urging him from a trot to a canter, I shook my head, as if to shake the insecurities from my brain. I had to get it together. This was just practice. We could do this. I needed to pretend that no one was watching and it was just Beau and me.

"Let's go," I said in a whisper to Beau.

I pointed him toward the first cross rail, and he hopped over the center with ease. I sat deep in the saddle, rocking to his canter as we eased into a slow turn and headed for the next jump.

We reached it, and Beau tucked his forelegs under his body, and we went up, up, up. I crouched into the two-point position, lifting my butt out of the saddle and sliding my hands forward along his neck. He landed well on the other side of the vertical, and I looked ahead to the oxer.

Oxers were one of my favorite kinds of jumps. They were made of two verticals that were placed one behind the other to create a spread. The spread could grow wider depending on difficulty. But I had to be careful not to let Beau knock the first pole on takeoff or hit the other pole on the landing.

I could feel Selly's and Nina's eyes on me. Strides before the jump, I let my gaze flick to my teammates. *No, focus!* I yelled at myself. I pulled my gaze back between Beau's ears, but it was too late. The jump rushed at us. Beau launched into the air a half second too late—he'd felt my distraction, and he'd stopped paying attention too.

We landed safely on the other side without clipping the poles, but we'd gotten lucky. If the rails had been higher and the spread wider, we would have knocked a rail, no question. I bounced a bit in the saddle on landing, annoyed at myself for losing focus. I couldn't do that for a second on a jump course. That was Basic Jumping 101, and I knew better.

Gritting my teeth, I pushed all thoughts of my teammates out of my head. I listened to Beau's rhythmic breathing and his hooves striking the dirt as we popped over the blue-and-white poles of the fourth jump before I eased him up a bit to roll back and clear the fifth jump.

Five down, two to go.

I gave him a bit more rein, letting him pick up the pace as we cantered down the end of the arena and came around to the tallest vertical. As we approached the jump, I started counting down in my head.

Three, two, one, *now!*

On *now*, I lifted out of the saddle and leaned forward as Beau rose into the air. It felt like flying. This was the most exhilarating feeling in the entire world. Beau landed with room to spare on the other side, and we headed for the final jump. As Beau cantered toward the oxer, I narrowed my gaze between his ears—one forward, one back—and waited for the right second.

We reached the oxer, and Beau rocked back on his forelegs, launching himself into the air. My seat was out of the saddle, my hands steady, and I gave him rein to stretch. We soared through the air before cleanly landing on the other side.

Yes! I grinned, sitting down in the saddle and letting Beau canter for a few strides. It hadn't been a perfect ride, but I'd managed to pull it together after my wobble early in the course.

"Nice job, boy," I told Beau.

As I slowed him from a canter to a trot, I leaned forward and patted his neck. He'd been great—I'd been the one who had messed up.

"Good ride!" Thea called. She and the rest of the team clapped. It had been a good ride, but I'd wanted it to be great. *Gorgeous*, even.

We trotted back to my teammates and Rebecca, and Selly

smirked as she leaned over to whisper to Nina. I forced myself not to react as I angled Beau next to Thea and Chaos. Steeling myself, I looked at my teammates.

"Let's start with Keir," Rebecca said.

He smiled at me, and his dark brown eyes met mine. "You and Beau are so in tune," he said. "It's really great to watch. The only downside of that is, you wobbled for a second and so did he. He felt you stop paying attention, so he did the same. But it was only one jump!" Keir said quickly. "Otherwise, that was an awesome ride, Abs."

I'd take that. "Thanks, Keir."

Rebecca nodded to Selly next. I fought to keep a placid expression on my face and not let myself react to whatever harshness she was surely about to spew at me.

"Keir's right," Selly said. She shrugged one shoulder. "You're so in tune with Beau that he follows your every move, which is great if you're focused, but if you're not?" She shook her head. "If you hadn't managed to get your concentration back, the entire course would have been a disaster. I'd work on keeping your eyes where they belong."

I huffed, blowing out an irritated breath.

"Abby," Rebecca warned.

I winced, trying to drop my attitude.

"Thanks, Selly," I said, my tone a bit flat. I didn't defend myself, though. We were supposed to be open and listen to feedback and not be defensive when others were trying to help. But Selly hadn't intended to be helpful, and we all knew that.

"Selly," Rebecca said in a warning tone. "Let's keep the attitude out of critiques, okay? We're here to help and lift one another up on this team."

Selly bowed her head, and when she looked up at Rebecca, her eyes were wide. "I'm so sorry, Rebecca," she said. "I'm just *so* passionate about this group. I want everyone to do well, and I get a bit too intense in my critiques."

I almost scoffed aloud. Surely, no one bought that.

"I do understand that," Rebecca said. "But be mindful of your tone going forward."

"I will," Selly promised. When Rebecca looked away, Selly smiled at me.

I glanced at Thea, and we both rolled our eyes. Selly knew how to turn on the charm around the people who mattered, I'd give her that.

"Go ahead, Emery," Rebecca said.

Please be as nice to me as I was to you, I thought as I looked at my stepsister.

"That was a strong ride," Emery said, smiling at me. "I really like watching you and Beau. You two seem well-matched, and he's such a solid jumper. He listened to all your cues and was able to make it cleanly over the jump when you lost focus for a second. Watch your chin, though. You dropped it a lot."

Whew.

I don't know why I'd expected Emery to be, well, like Selly. Emery wasn't a mean person. She hadn't said one bad word about me or to me. Like, ever.

"Thank you," I said, smiling. Her criticism had been helpful, and she was right—I *had* dropped my chin.

The rest of my teammates hurried through their critiques as dark, thick clouds began to roll in as a storm approached.

"Your teammates were spot-on," Rebecca said, nodding to me. "It was a solid ride, but you have to stay focused. Your chin was dropped, and you gripped with your knees. You lost contact with your entire right leg and left it swinging. That greatly decreases your security in the saddle, which you know. So we're going to make sure we work on that."

I flushed three shades of pink—I could feel it. Rebecca

was right. Ugh. I knew better than to pinch with my knees. Taking a deep breath, I tried to remind myself that was why I was on this team—to get better. That wouldn't happen if no one pointed out my faults. I had between now and Friday to practice, practice, practice.

The Suspect List

AFTER DINNER VIVI AND I WENT BACK to our room, and she shut our door behind us. Rain pelted the windows, which made me feel cozy. We'd made some green tea with lemon—a Lauren Towers staple rec—and I took a sip of mine.

"Ready to brainstorm Truth X. Poser suspects?" she asked me.

I nodded. "So ready."

Vivi grabbed a dry-erase marker for each of us, kept the blue one, and tossed me the purple. Our big dry-erase board hung to the right of Vivi's desk.

Vivi wrote *Truth X. Poser* at the top of the board, then turned to me. "Okay, so. Who all is on your riding team?"

"That's complicated," I said. "There's a big stable group with a bunch of smaller teams inside. We have younger kids, older riders, and people our age. I have all their names in the team directory, but I don't know everyone. Not even close. Oh, and? We have noncompetitive riders at the barn too."

"Lots of people you don't know," Vivi said. "That kind of eliminates them as suspects, right?"

I half shrugged. "I'd think so? I mean, why would they target someone they don't even know? That would be kind of pointless."

"So, who do you ride with?" Vivi asked. "Let's start there."

I ticked off each name on my fingers. "Selly. Nina. Keir. Emery. Thea."

"Is there anyone else you regularly talk to at the stable?" Vivi asked.

"Hmm . . ." It was hard to think on the spot. "Maia. But only sometimes. Maybe a couple of the other older riders if they come to demonstrate a technique or something to our team."

Vivi kept asking me questions, and she made list after list on the whiteboard. We had lists of whose stalls were around Beau's, people I'd seen that day even in passing, and anyone

Emery had been seen with. We had so many names floating all over the board. It was overwhelming.

"But none of these people hate me," I said. "Except Selly."

"It's usually not the most obvious person, though," Vivi said. "I learned that from watching detective shows with my mom this summer."

"That would make it too easy, huh?" I asked, taking a deep breath. "So, let's focus on the other people on my team. If we look at everyone I might have passed in the span of a day, it's too many people and no motive."

Vivi capped her marker and pulled her desk chair next to mine. We both sat in our chairs, staring up at the whiteboard.

"We've got Selly, Nina, Emery, Keir, and Thea," she said. "Let's talk about each one. Tell me if you've ever had problems with any of them. Obviously, I know you haven't had issues with Thea, since she's your other BFF, but it can't hurt to talk through everyone."

"I don't know where to start with Selly," I said. "She's disliked me since last year." I thought back to the first moment we'd met. "She sees Saddlehill and the stable as her territories. No one has ever challenged her on that either."

"Until you," Vivi said.

"Yup. I came to Foxbury, and I want to be the best rider in my division. I have zero problem taking the crown from Selly. Except I haven't succeeded. Yet."

Vivi reached over and squeezed my hand. "Hey, nothing's over! You've still got plenty of time to take it from her. New year, new show season."

I blinked, seeing my entire fall-from-grace performance at the Fieldcrest Classic flash before my eyes. Everyone had been counting on me to sweep. I'd been so sure I would, and so had my dad. He'd even taken time off work—which he never did—to come watch me. And I'd failed. Horribly. I'd fallen flat on my face. Not literally, but it had sure felt like it at the time, when my body had slammed to the ground during cross-country. Taking the crown from Selly seemed far away right now after everything that had happened.

"Anyway," I said, snapping out of my memory. "Selly is Selly. We've never been friends and never will be. She does everything with a smile and tries to make you feel like she's doing you a favor when she's being mean to you."

"Maybe we do need to look at her," Vivi said. She got up and wrote *Never liked Abby. Not friends* next to Selly's name. "What if it's one of those 'so obvious it has to be true' situations?"

"It could be," I said. "Nina and I used to talk once in a while last year, but after she became Selly's bestie? Forget it. She'll never tell me anything about Selly if she was somehow involved."

"Nina might talk to me. She's in my history class, so I'll see what I can get out of her. I doubt it will be much, but I'll try."

"Unless Nina is the TXP," I said. But I frowned as I said the words. "It doesn't feel like something Nina would do, though. Plus, we were friendly for so long."

"That's true, you were. I'll talk to her just in case."

"Thanks," I said. "And thank you for all this." I gestured toward the whiteboard. "Let's take a break. I know it's not exactly a super-fun activity to do."

Vivi waved off my comment. "Oh, please. This is way better than starting the reading for our English class."

"Really? You mean you don't want to learn about Mr. William Shakespeare for the ninety-seventh time?"

Vivi moaned. "We just studied that dude last year. We'll never escape him, I swear."

I sighed. "This year I'm going for it. I'm going to beg and ask if we can read Elizabeth Acevedo. Her poetry puts Shakespeare's to shame."

"Ooh, yes, please! I'll even go with you when you ask Ms.

Hezel. Then I could tell her just how important books are to me."

"You mean how you always carry an e-reader, a charging cord, and a paperback copy in case you can't reach a charger and your battery dies?"

Vivi nodded with a pretend-serious expression. "Exactly. You know me."

Vivi was as big of a reader as I was, if not more, which was saying something. She'd introduced me to some of my favorite authors too.

"I do," I said. "Quite well, actually."

She nodded. "And reading those ghost-hunting books together over the summer was one of my favorite things I did. Now we can read together and not have to discuss them over text or FaceTime!"

"I can't wait." I rolled my shoulders, trying to ease the tension out of them.

Vivi scooted her chair closer to mine and bumped my shin with her foot. "I want to figure this out too. Maybe I'll have a second career as a detective when I'm older, in addition to acting."

"Or maybe you'll get a role playing a detective," I said. "Then all of this was good character research."

"Now you're thinking!" Vivi laughed as she swiped her phone off her desk. She busily tapped the screen.

"What are you doing?"

"Getting a proper detective outfit, of course!"

I laughed. For the millionth time since I'd met her, I felt grateful to have Vivi in my life. She was my best friend, aside from Thea, and she was the one who was going to help me crack this case.

I watched her smile as she browsed for an outfit, and a tiny part of me wanted to tell her the whole truth. I felt so guilty that she was trying to help solve this mystery without having all the info. But I couldn't. I just couldn't do it. I didn't want to have her look at me in a different way after what I'd done. Not when my mistake had cost Selly so much.

I grabbed my own phone and zoomed in on the white-board. I snapped a pic and pulled up my texts with Emery.

We're gonna figure this out ☺, I texted her, along with the picture. This way, she could see our notes about my relationship with Selly without my having to say anything bad about her.

Now, I just had to believe that Vivi and I could solve this mystery. And I had to make sure we did before the TXP broadcasted my secret for everyone to know.

It Must Be Love

TUESDAY MORNING WAS OFF TO A MUCH better start than Monday's had been. No texts or emails from the TXP. And? I'd woken up to a text from Dad. He'd sent it just to me, saying good morning and to have a great day. I'd been smiley all through first-period study hall.

Now I walked into Mr. Kemp's world history class and took my seat. Mr. Kemp was already one of my favorite teachers, and it was only the second day of classes. Sure, he was friendly and all, but the main reason I liked coming to this classroom?

His plants.

Mr. Kemp's classroom had a giant bay window. He'd put plants all along the large ledge in pots of various sizes and a rainbow of colors. He had a great collection of zoo animal planters—my favorite being the giraffe.

His desk had plants too. Tiny succulents in Pokémon planters that were shaped like Oddishes. I had a Bulbasaur one, but I hadn't seen the Oddish before, so I knew exactly what I'd spend future birthday money on.

Thea walked into the classroom and slid into her seat next to me.

"Uh-oh," she said.

"What?"

"You have that look on your face. That dreamy 'in love' look."

"I do not! But if I did, why 'uh-oh'?" I asked.

"Because I saw what you were staring at. Abby, repeat after me."

I rolled my eyes but grinned. "Go on."

"I, Abby St. Clair," Thea said.

"I, Abby St. Clair," I repeated, shaking my head.

"Do not need."

"Do not need," I said.

"Another plant. Or my room will become a jungle, and the plants will start to overtake me in my sleep. And then I'll be lost forever to a tangle of greenery, and no one will be able to find my body."

I laughed. "Oh, *stop*! That's so not true. My room is nowhere near a jungle! Hello, Vivi would have told me if it was. She's a very spoiled person. She wouldn't live in a jungle."

Thea arched an eyebrow, and I could see her struggle to hold back a laugh. "How many plants do you have?"

I leaned back in my chair, pretending to think even though I knew the answer. "Seven."

"Abby."

"It's true! But I might have my eye on three more succulents. Maybe!"

Thea folded her arms across her chest. "See? You're trying to hide how many you really have. That signals a problem."

I laughed again. "Does n—"

"Oh, please." Selly took a seat behind me. I hadn't even heard her walk into the classroom. "We do not have time to list all of Abby's problems. That would take this entire period."

I stiffened. Did Selly have to insert herself into every conversation? No one was talking to her.

"It was a joke," I said flatly. "You know, a thing that's funny?"

Selly smirked. "Oh, like your face? Or funny like how you're trying to unmask the Truth X. Poser?"

Thea made a noise. "Can you not, Selly? Seriously. Go bother someone else."

"Aw, calm down, guard dog," Selly said, smoothing her pink tee. Now she sounded bored. "You're always defending your little bestie."

I gritted my teeth. "Don't call Thea a dog. And I don't need anyone to defend me. Especially against your boring comments."

Selly's brown eyes narrowed, and a hint of color bloomed in her cheeks. Before she could respond, Mr. Kemp walked into the room.

I turned around to face the front of the room, trying to shake off my annoyance. I knew better than to let her get to me. Last year she'd tormented me so much that I'd spent the first couple of months here wondering if I should pack up and go home. But Dad had come to visit during one of my worst bouts of anxiety caused by Selly. He had offered to go to the dean to talk about Selly's behavior, but I'd been fully against that idea—it would only make things worse. He'd also brought up the idea of me coming back home, but if I went, she'd feel like what she'd done was okay, and she'd do it to the next person.

I didn't want Selly to ever think her mean-girl antics worked. So I stayed. I threw myself into classes and riding. I met Thea and Vivi, and I refused to give up my two best friends because of Selly. So Thea and I stuck together at lessons. During classes I shared with Selly, I hung with Vivi if possible. Or anyone else that I knew. I'd become an expert at dodging Selly most of the time. But times like this, when I couldn't, I was also learning how to throw stuff right back at her and not just take it. I didn't ever want to become like her, though, so it was a balancing act.

"Good morning, friends!" Mr. Kemp said, greeting us with a smile. He was a young teacher like Ms. Foster, and he always had a smile on his face. He pushed his blue-framed glasses up his nose, looking around at all of us. When he called us "friends," I felt as though he meant it.

"Good morning!" we all said back.

"I'm so happy to see all your faces again," Mr. Kemp said. "It was wonderful to meet everyone yesterday. I'll do my best to remember names, but it's only the second day. So please kindly remind me if you speak during class."

While he took attendance, I opened my notes app and put the date on the top of a piece of paper in my world history notebook. For this class, I'd chosen a notebook with a bright green cover and tiny doodles of hearts and flowers all over it. I wasn't great at drawing flowers, but it was something I wanted to get better at doing. Especially since I loved plants so much.

"All right," Mr. Kemp said, "now that we've got that out of the way, I started grading your summer packets last night. Thank you all for your hard work. I'll finish grading the rest of them tonight, but let me say, I'm impressed by the work I've seen so far."

I smiled, crossing my fingers that my packet was one Mr. Kemp had graded already. The summer homework for this class hadn't been too bad. I'd done the required reading and had watched a video lecture that was supposed to prepare us for what was coming this year in Mr. Kemp's class. I'd always liked history, so I was sure this class wouldn't be a problem for me. Or I hoped it wouldn't be.

"Today I want to talk about the five themes of geography," Mr. Kemp said. "We covered those in your summer packet. Does anyone remember what they are?"

Shoot. What had I just thought about this class being a breeze? My mind went blank.

"Yes?" Mr. Kemp asked, nodding toward Selly.

"I'm Selly," she reminded him. "I can't remember all of them, but I know two. Region and place."

"Very good, Selly," Mr. Kemp said.

My hand shot into the air. Selly's answer had triggered my own memory. "Human interaction," I said when Mr. Kemp pointed to me. "Oh, I'm Abby."

But Mr. Kemp didn't nod at my response. Instead, he gave me a sympathetic smile. "So close, Abby. It's actually 'human-environment interaction.' But great try!"

Behind me, Selly snorted. Not loud enough for anyone but me to hear.

It was just one sort of wrong answer, I told myself. *You'll get the next one.*

Mr. Kemp called on Oliver next, and he easily listed the other two themes.

As the lesson went on, I busied myself with taking notes and tried to forget about Selly. Mr. Kemp's class flew by, and I was surprised when he told us it was almost time to get to our next class.

"But not without homework, of course," he said.

We groaned.

"It's only the second day," Oliver said.

Mr. Kemp bent down beside his desk and loaded his arms with a stack of magazines. "It's not going to be hard," he said, "promise." He put the magazines down on the empty table in front of the whiteboard. "In a minute, you're going to come up and grab a magazine. Then you may leave. Tonight I want you to go through your magazine—just random ones I've saved over the summer—and find me one example of each of the five themes we discussed. Once you find a theme, cut it out and label it. Bring it to class tomorrow. When you're done with the magazine, please drop it in the nearest recycling bin."

I scribbled down the assignment in my homework journal. It was only second period, but I had a feeling I'd have a lot of homework tonight. Teachers here weren't shy about assignments. I'd learned that lesson last year. After I'd packed my bag and grabbed a magazine, I waved goodbye to Thea, who had a different class next, and left.

Once I was outside, I pulled my phone out of my bag to text Vivi. Before I could tap her name, I noticed a new text from Emery.

Are you free after school? she asked. I wanted to talk to you about something. 😊

What was that about?

As I hurried down the sidewalk to math, I sent her a quick text back. Sure! Meet me at the center fountain at 3?

She texted back immediately. Cool! See you then.

By the time I reached the math building, I'd been so lost in thought wondering what Emery wanted to talk about that I'd completely forgotten to text Vivi. I needed the rest of classes to hurry up so I could find out what Emery wanted to talk about. Only a few more hours, and I'd find out.

Cryptic Text

THANKFULLY, I WAS SO DISTRACTED BY wondering what Emery wanted that it helped the day go by fast. At lunch, I'd grabbed my usual seat next to Thea and Vivi and had blurted out how Emery wanted to talk after classes. They'd both shared my curiosity and, like me, wished Emery had the same lunch period so we could talk sooner. But nope, we had to wait until the end of the school day to talk. At least the time had finally come.

I'd promised Thea I'd fill her in later when we groomed our horses. Vivi was busy now with theater stuff, so I'd tell her how it went when she was done. We'd decided to grab Chinese food tonight and do homework together.

My last class of the day had been gym, so I'd come straight from there to the center fountain. I'd picked an iron bench under a shady tree and stretched my legs as I sat and waited for Emery. This fountain—one of many—was my favorite on campus. It had a giant reflection pool and a dozen streams of water shooting into the air at various heights. A ledge ran around the fountain's edge, and sometimes I'd sit there and let the fountain mist blow over me.

I scrolled social media and started looking at back-to-school pics from my friends just as Emery walked up to me.

"Hey!" she said, giving me a smile. "Thanks for meeting me."

"No problem. It's nice to sit outside for a minute and chill."

"I totally know what you mean. I ran from class to class today, and I've still got to change and go groom Bliss. So yeah, I'm excited to sit for a moment too."

I patted the other end of the bench. "You're still standing."

Laughing, Emery sat and turned toward me, managing to sit cross-legged with one knee up against the back of the bench. "I'm fried from today. As evidenced by my talking about sitting while standing."

"It will get easier. It doesn't seem like it right now, especially when the week isn't even halfway over yet. But you'll get used to the schedule."

Emery chewed on her bottom lip. "How long did it take you?"

I thought about it for a few seconds. "Honestly, it probably took until close to Thanksgiving break before I fully felt at home. I know that sounds like a long time and it kind of is, but I was also so busy that I didn't give myself enough time to actually settle in. Does that even make sense?"

Emery nodded. "It does. You don't have time to take it all in because things are happening at one hundred miles per hour. That's how I felt today, anyway."

I nodded. She was exactly right.

"I didn't have time to have a 'wow, I'm at Saddlehill' moment on Monday because I was too busy," she continued, "and too worried about finding all my classes and not getting lost. I figured I'd get to have that moment today—the one where I kind of sat back, looked around, and felt present."

"But you were still too busy, huh?"

"So busy! I don't hate it, though. At my old school, the day used to drag sometimes. By lunch, I would be half-asleep because I was bored. I know it's only the second day, but I honestly wasn't bored once."

"The teachers here are pretty special," I said. "I thought I got lucky last year with all good teachers, but after meeting my teachers this year? It's not luck. Saddlehill teachers care about us, and they want us to learn as bad as they want to teach us." I laughed. "I sound like part of the brochure!"

Emery laughed but waved a hand. "No, you're good. It's comforting to hear that you love all your teachers too. I think you'd have to extra love your job if you wanted to teach here, anyway. Living on campus and all that."

I nodded. "For sure. Did you walk by any of the faculty cottages yet?"

Emery shook her head. "Not yet. Between classes and getting settled in, there's been no time."

"Understandable," I said. "When things settle down, text me. We can walk by faculty row, where the bulk of their houses are. You'll see how cute each of the teachers make their front yards. It's kind of an unofficial competition among them, and they really get into it on holidays."

Emery smiled. "That would be fun!" She shifted on the bench. "And hey, sorry I was cryptic before when I texted you."

I couldn't help but laugh. "Funny you use that word. Because I was thinking that exactly when I got your text."

She shook her head. "I know better than to send texts like that! It's nothing bad, I promise. I wanted to talk to you about the Truth X. Poser."

"What's up?" My shoulders relaxed at her promise of no bad news.

"I looked at the photo you sent me last night. Like, for a long time. I know that whiteboard took you and Vivi hours."

I nodded. "It did. We're going through every person in our immediate riding group, talking about other people on the team, and even writing down names of noncompetitive riders who could have been at the stable." I blew out a breath. "It's so open, though. There are so many people. But who did it? Who is coming after me?"

Emery tucked a lock of hair behind her ear. "I wish we knew. I still believe you that the video was edited, by the way. And yes, seeing you putting all that time into figuring it out with Vivi made it even clearer that you didn't do it."

"Good," I said. "I'm glad you still think that."

"After seeing how busy I've been the past two days, I know you're just as stressed," she said. "So I think you shouldn't worry about uncovering the Truth X. Poser's identity anymore."

I tilted my head to look at her. "Really? You don't want to know who did this?"

"Oh, I do! But I saw the board. I know how many names there are, and you even said how much time that took. I don't want you to feel like you have to do it to prove something to me."

"I don't," I said. "I want to know who did this to me. To us. But really to me. It's . . . *unsettling,* to say the least. To know that someone wants to mess with me so bad. I feel like I can't trust anyone. Besides Vivi and Thea. And you," I added quickly. "It kind of goes without saying."

Emery nodded, giving me a quick smile. "If you're sure," she said. "But please don't feel like you *have* to do anything."

I smiled back. "Thanks for talking to me about this. But listen, Vivi already went shopping for a detective hat, so there's no way I can tell her the plan is off."

Emery burst into laughter. "What the heck is a detective hat?" she asked, laughing again once she got the question out. "Wait, tell me she ordered one of those super-old-fashioned hats, the ones with little propellers on them?" She clasped her hands together in front of her. "That would make my *life.*"

I laughed along with her. "I didn't actually see the hat she ordered," I said. "All I know is she told me she was buying one."

"So there's still hope that it could be that kind of hat," Emery said. "Promise you'll text me when it gets here? I need to see it."

"Oh, I promise. You'll be the first one I text." I checked the time, sighing. "I'm not trying to be rude, but I have to get changed and get to the stable soon."

Emery nodded and jumped off the bench. "Me too. Thanks again for talking to me." She looked as if she wanted to say something else, but instead, she just smiled.

With that, we said our goodbyes and headed in opposite directions, and I couldn't help but think how nice it was that she was looking out for me.

Let's Get It Started

AWHILE LATER, I HEADED TO THE indoor arena for Rebecca's unmounted meeting. The arena buzzed with riders, from newly-allowed-on-the-team fourth graders to high school seniors. Our IPL had a team of Western riders too, but they were coached by different instructors, and their unmounted meeting was on another day.

Last year, when I'd started attending my first unmounted meetings, I thought for sure I'd be sad not to be on horseback while at the stable. But that hadn't been the case at all. I loved learning anything and everything about horses, and our unmounted meetings from last year had taught me so much.

My favorite unmounted activity? The quiz bowls, where we got to square off against each other and test our horse knowledge. I couldn't wait to become an even smarter horse nerd this year.

I wandered over toward the middle of the arena, where I spotted Thea. She looked up from her phone, smiling.

Most of the riders here had grouped themselves loosely by age. The younger kids had gathered toward the front of the arena, my friends and I were sort of in the middle, and the older kids were in the back.

We waited for Rebecca, and I bit back a groan when Selly and Nina walked over to Thea and me.

"This is so boring," Selly said, stifling a yawn. "I don't know why we had to have an unmounted meeting today. We should be on horseback, you know, practicing." She shrugged. "But it's not like I have any competition anyway in our group." She rolled her eyes. "I wish Maia and her friends rode with us all the time."

"Excuse you," Nina said. "You've got competition."

Selly looked over her shoulder twice. "Where?" she asked.

Nina sighed. "I can't with you." There was no anger in her tone, though.

It still bugged me to see Nina so close to Selly. I couldn't stomach Selly, and she felt the same about me. The difference between us? Selly had probably badgered Nina about liking me until Nina had given up and quit hanging out with me. I'd never said a bad word about Selly to Nina.

"No, I'm serious," Selly said. "If you see my competition, please point them out."

Nina reached over and whacked Selly's upper arm. *"Stop!"*

They giggled, and I stood there not saying a word. Across the arena, I spotted Emery walking in, and I almost sighed with relief. I whispered to Thea that I'd be right back and went over by Emery. She'd found Wren and Zoe, and the three sixth graders looked up at me with smiles when I came over.

"Hey," I said. "Exciting day, huh? We get to talk about the show season."

The girls nodded.

"I'm so ready for it to start," Wren said. "I practiced so much this summer."

"You got a new horse, right?" I asked her.

She nodded. "I did! A Holsteiner. He's really cute."

"What did you sign up for this year?" I asked Zoe. The petite sixth grader was one to watch too. She was one of the best young riders in our group.

"I considered doing only dressage," she said, "but then I thought about it more. I want to take jumper classes too. It's new for me, so I have to start at the intro classes. But I jumped a bit over summer break and really liked it."

"That's so cool," I said. "I'm glad you found something new that you liked."

"How about you?" Emery asked me. "I mean, I think I know the answer, but I'm asking anyway."

"Honestly, it wasn't as set for me as you might think. I considered focusing on hunt seat only this year. I love it—both on the flat and over fences. But I adore eventing so much that I didn't want to give it up. So I'm sticking with eventing."

Just thinking about a three-day weekend show sent chills up and down my spine. One day for dressage, one for show jumping, and one for cross-country.

"I feel you on that," Emery said. "That's what I decided too. Dressage is my weakest area, but I don't want to stop competing in it because I learn so much from it and become a better rider by doing it."

We all fell silent, taking our seats on the bleachers, when Rebecca walked into the arena, tablet in hand. She put it down on a banquet table that had been erected in front of the bleachers and smoothed her gray polo with one hand.

"Hello, hello," Rebecca said. "I hope you're all having a great afternoon!"

My afternoon was definitely looking up now that we were able to talk about the show season.

"Thank you all for meeting today," Rebecca said. "We'll get right to it since we're busy. As you all know, I want our teams to qualify for nationals this year. On top of that, I want each of you as individuals to do well and take home the top spots. But to do well as an individual rider means to do well on a team. So I expect nothing less than teamwork one hundred percent of this show season. Got it?"

"Got it," we said back.

Rebecca nodded. "I will say this every year: If you're not willing to be a good teammate? Then riding for me isn't going to work. I expect you to support your fellow riders. No matter what their riding level or discipline of choice. We all must work together, or we won't go anywhere. Anyone who doesn't have the best interest of the team at heart will not ride for me." Rebecca looked over our small crowd, almost as if she was eyeing each one of us.

"So, as a group, we're going to be attending multiple shows this season. Your total scores from your shows and the classes you take will either advance you to area and regional championships, or they won't. It depends on your rides, and I hope those take you all the way to nationals."

Goose bumps popped up my arms. All I wanted was to go to nationals this season. No. Scratch that. All I wanted was to *win*.

Last year, it had been crushing to do decent all season and then have it all go downhill, starting with the Fieldcrest Classic. But that was something I'd been working on putting behind me. This show season was the fresh start I needed.

More than anything, I wanted to make my dad proud, and a win would do that. I glanced over at Emery. *Especially now,* I thought. *You have to make him proud when she's so good.* I pulled myself out of my thoughts and focused on Rebecca. Hopefully, the rest of the week would go by fast, and it would be Friday before I knew it.

"I'm going to be attending a lot of shows between now and the end of show season," Rebecca said. "That will give you the opportunity to have a few choices and some flexibility to pick dates that work best for you. We'll also talk with your teachers to make sure these dates work for everyone."

Next week I'd take the schedule to my teachers and talk to them about my plans. Thankfully, they would help make sure I'd be able to keep up with all my classes while still allowing me to show often.

"I'm going to pass out the schedules, and you'll see what shows I'll be attending," Rebecca said. "Those of you who are going to this weekend's show already have that date locked in, but the rest of the season is open."

We all nodded. As Rebecca handed out the paperwork, I looked over at Thea with a grin on my face. She met my gaze with a matching smile.

Once everyone had schedules, Rebecca cleared her throat. "Now, I want you each to think about a few questions."

"Is one 'How are we going to beat Canterwood?'" Keir called, causing several cheers to break out among the other riders.

Rebecca laughed. "I mean, yes, that's a valid and legit question, Keir. But the ones I had in mind are: What do you want from yourself this show season? What is within your control to help you get what you want? What steps are you going to take to get to your end goal?"

Zoe raised her hand. "What do you mean, though? Within our control?"

"Well, unfortunately, you can't always control how your horse might act. But you can control how *you* react if there's a spook or a shy or a knocked rail."

"I want to sweep in my division," Selly said. "That's within my control. I can win if I work hard enough."

I surprised myself by nodding to what Selly said.

"Hard work is certainly an important factor," Rebecca said. "But it's not the only thing that determines a championship win. It's going to take a combination of timing, luck, talent, and a good rapport with your horse. So let's rephrase one of my questions. What exact steps are you going to take to give yourself the best possible shot at doing well this season?"

Again, Selly started to answer, but Rebecca raised a hand. "Don't answer that aloud. I want you to really think about it over the next few days."

While Rebecca talked us through the rest of the plan for this week, my mind drifted to her questions. And for once, I found myself in complete alignment with Selly. I wanted to win in my division, and I believed I could if I worked hard enough.

It felt as though a countdown clock had started to tick in my head: I had three days until my show season started. Three days until I'd start to test my plan to win.

Miss Me?

A SHORT WHILE LATER, I GRABBED
Beau's grooming kit and took him out of his stall.
Thea and I were meeting under the big shady oaks
behind the stable. It was one of our favorite spots to groom
them. Plus, it was private. I'd learned my lesson about talking
inside the stable and potentially having someone listen in.

My phone buzzed, and I fished it out of my pocket.

"Hi, Dad!" I answered.

"Hey, hon. It's so good to hear your voice. I miss you so
much!"

"Miss you, too. It feels like I've been gone forever and also not long at all."

"I completely agree with that," he said, "which is why I'm calling. I was supposed to go on a business trip this weekend, but it got postponed. What do you think if I came to your show on Saturday? I can't make it for Friday's dressage, but I can be there for show jumping and probably cross-country on Sunday. I could get a nearby hotel room, and we could hang out after your rides."

"Really?" I asked. "Just us?" I was desperate for alone time with my dad. This past summer had been all about the June wedding, moving into the Flynns' house, and Dad and Natalie spending time together as a new couple. I needed my dad too, and he'd spent *plenty* of time with Emery lately.

"Just us," he confirmed. "It'll be good to spend time with you, Abs. But only if you don't already have plans after the show. It's your first full weekend back at school, so if you have things to do—tell me. It won't hurt my feelings."

"I don't have any plans! So, yes, please come!"

Dad laughed. "All right, then. I'll text you on Friday night when I get in and join up with Natalie."

Oh. Natalie. "I thought it was just us," I said.

"It is. She's having a girls' weekend with Emery and watching her compete."

"Ohhh, okay." That worked out pretty perfectly, actually. Emery would have her mom, and I got my dad.

"Be thinking about what you want to do for dinner on Saturday, okay?"

I smiled, patting Beau's neck with my free hand. "You got it."

We said our goodbyes and hung up just as Thea led Chaos up to the other tie ring.

"What's up?" she asked me, staring. "I haven't seen you smile that hard in a long time!"

"That was my dad," I said. "He's coming to town on Friday night, and he wants to hang out after I ride on Saturday."

"No Emery?" Thea asked.

"No Emery. She's going to be with Natalie."

A big grin stretched across Thea's face. "I'm so happy for you. No offense to Emery, because she does seem really nice. But I know how much you've missed your dad."

Reaching for a dandy brush, I nodded. "I like Emery, and you know that I do. It's been hard, though. I was an only child for my entire life until now. After my mom left, it was me and my dad. For years. I've always shared him with his work but not with other people. Does that even make sense?"

Thea nodded as she whisked dust from Chaos's shiny coat. "It does. I'd need one-on-one time with my dad too, if I were in your shoes."

Thea always made me feel better about this whole insta-fam thing. Her own parents were divorced, so she understood complicated family dynamics.

"So, tell me all about your talk with Emery," Thea said. "I've been dying to know."

As we groomed our horses, I filled her in. Like me, Thea didn't think I should give up on uncovering the TXP's identity.

"At this point, Vivi's a step away from buying a big handlebar mustache to go with her detective hat," I said, "so there's no way I'm missing *that*."

We cracked up.

After the horses were groomed, we went our separate ways and I led Beau back to his stall. As I headed down the aisle, I hurried past Ember's stall when I saw Selly inside. Talking to her was the last thing I wanted to do.

I took my time feeding and watering Beau and looked

over his feed schedule for the rest of the week. I wanted to make sure he had everything he needed to be in top shape for the show season. While I compared his food to an article I'd read about essential nutrients, I made a list on my phone of a couple of vitamin supplements to ask Rebecca about later.

My phone chimed, and I figured it was Dad. Maybe he'd looked into some options for dinner. My breath caught when I looked at the screen and saw a new text.

Unknown sender: You need to stop digging. I already warned you once. But thanks for the whiteboard dedicated to me! 😀

Then a photo appeared of the whiteboard and a black-gloved hand making a thumbs-up.

27

Violated

I SUCKED IN A BREATH, MY HEART hammering in my chest. Who was in my room? I tore off out of the stable and managed to snag a seat in one of the waiting buses, willing it to go faster as we made our way to campus—not even waiting to grab my usual bus with Thea. I'd make it up to her later.

Back at Saddlehill, I ran down the sidewalk, dodging a group of boys who walked toward me.

"Hey, watch it!" one yelled after me as I nearly rammed

into him. But I didn't stop or turn around to apologize.

Someone had been in our room.

Or *was* in our room.

I needed to get there before they left. *Just cut through the grass!* I yelled to myself. I'd get detention if I got caught, but oh well, this was too important. I darted off the sidewalk, stepped onto the lawn, and kept running. Teachers would have to catch me to give me detention.

Breathing hard, I finally reached Amherst's yard and hurried up the steps and into the house. I gulped, trying to slow my ragged breaths. Thanks for nothing, runs I did all summer! Should I wait here and hope to catch whoever it was leaving the house? Or go to my room? I stood there for a second, trying to decide, then went for it and headed for the stairs.

My hands shook as I turned the doorknob to our room and peered inside.

No one was there.

I yanked open my closet door, then Vivi's, half expecting to find the Truth X. Poser hiding inside. But no. Everything was untouched as far as I could tell.

Everything except . . . I stepped closer to our whiteboard. Someone had slashed a giant *X* across the board. They'd keyed it right to the backing.

Anger pulsed through my veins. Someone had already taped me without my consent. And now? They'd been in my personal space. My room. My sacred space on campus that was *mine*. Mine and Vivi's.

I left my room, slamming the door behind me, and headed back downstairs to the common room, where I found two older girls on the couch eating strawberry yogurts.

"Sorry to bother you," I said, "but did you see anyone in our house who doesn't live here?"

"When?" the redheaded girl asked.

"Like, in the last hour," I said. "I don't know if they came in here or only went to the second floor."

Both girls shook their heads.

"Sorry," one of them said. "I didn't see anyone."

"Thanks anyway," I said.

I went around the rest of the house, knocked on all the closed doors, and asked everyone who was there if they'd seen a stranger in Amherst. But no one had. Most of them had been out at extracurriculars. The few students here had been in their rooms doing homework.

Great.

I dragged myself upstairs and back into my room, flopping onto our gray chaise lounge chair.

How had anyone gotten into our room? Most of us—Vivi and me included—kept our dorm room doors unlocked because the door to Amherst was locked. So no one but our own housemates could get in without a key. Or without someone letting them in.

My head snapped up when the doorknob turned.

"Hello, hello," Vivi said, smiling at me as she came inside. Her smile faded when she got a look at me. "What happened?"

"Look at our whiteboard," I said. "Then look at this."

I pulled up the text and the photo.

Vivi stepped over to look at the board and did exactly what I'd done—she touched the giant *X*. "Why did you—?"

I shook my head. "I didn't. The Truth X. Poser did." I showed her the text and pic. "They sent me that while I was at the stable. I got on the bus, then ran here—literally—and must have just missed them."

"Oh my god," Vivi said. She sank down into her desk chair. "Did anyone else see them?"

"No. I already asked around."

"Crap." Vivi's mouth drooped, and she rubbed her forehead.

"I know. They came into our room, V. Into our room!" I balled my hands into fists. "That's so messed up. It was bad enough that they faked that video of me. Now? They took it one step further and came into our space."

Vivi chewed on her thumbnail. "Maybe we should talk to Molly."

"No way," I said. "That will make it worse if we tattle. How well do you think that will go once they find out we told on them to our RA?"

"Ugh. You're probably right."

"I wish we could tell Molly. But it would only make the TXP angry. Besides, they must really be worried that we're getting close to their identity."

Vivi tilted her head. "Why do you think that?"

"They took a big risk by coming here," I said, "and getting into our room. I don't know, but I'd think someone would only do that if they really, really wanted to scare us off."

"That's a good point," Vivi said slowly. "If you're caught trespassing in another student's room, you'll get expelled. Or put on probation at the very least. Anyone could have seen them in this house."

"And how did they get in?"

Vivi leaned back in her chair. "Right. How did they?"

I ticked off the options on my fingers. "They either got a key somehow or someone let them in."

"Or an Amherst resident didn't lock the front door," Vivi said. "I forgot the other day."

Ugh. That realization threw another option at me.

"That could have been it, huh?" I asked. "No one here saw anyone. At least, none of the people I talked to. If someone left the door unlocked, then yikes. It really could have been easy for someone to sneak inside without a key."

"Unless they stole a key from someone," Vivi said. She scrubbed her face with her hand. "So many options, from people to motive to how they got in."

"Or," I said, "they live here."

"It's got to be Selly," Vivi said. "She lives here. She has motive. She's a jerk!"

I shook my head. "It wasn't her. I saw her at the stable before I came here. I walked right past her."

"Shoot." Vivi blew out a breath. "I'm out of ideas now."

"I'm not giving up," I said. "Especially not now. Not after they let themselves into our room and touched our stuff."

Vivi shook her head. "Oh, me neither! We're going to figure this thing out. I know it."

"We are smart, capable, and determined humans," I said.

Vivi reached over to fist-bump me, making me chuckle. "Absolutely. The TXP is going to regret messing with us."

Vivi and I locked eyes, both of us nodding. We were going to figure this out. No matter what. We'd have to be more careful with how we went about it, but so be it. The Truth X. Poser was going to be unmasked. I'd make sure of it.

Emotional Support
Towel

BY WEDNESDAY AFTERNOON, I WAS
exhausted. Besides the stress of TXP striking again,
I was back into the routine of getting up early, fit-
ting in homework and riding, and still making time to see my
friends. It was rough.

I rubbed my eyes—they burned from staying up way too
late with Vivi last night. We'd taken down our whiteboard,
flipped it around, and tacked sheets of paper onto the back.
I'd written *TXP* in big letters across one sheet of paper and
had put that at the top. While we used the whiteboard as a

makeshift corkboard, we'd gone online and ordered a new whiteboard. It would be here tomorrow. *Take that, TXP,* I thought.

"Would it make me old if I wanted to nap?" Vivi asked from her spot on her bed. She was lying on her side, watching me as I watered my plants and looked them over.

"No way," I said. "Only because I want to take one too, and I don't want you to call *me* old."

She laughed. "Fair enough."

Our phones chimed at the exact same time.

Anxiety swept through me, and I almost tripped over my backpack as I hurried to my desk to grab my phone.

But Vivi had hers first. "It's just Thea. Nothing bad!"

"Whew." I hated how even the sound of my own phone scared me now. The jolt of anxiety I felt when I saw a new text or email. Or heard my phone buzz or chime. I'd thought about silencing it, but I knew I'd worry imagining what was there waiting for me when I checked it.

I looked at my screen and opened my texts. It was a message to Vivi and me in our group chat with Thea.

Thea: I'm hot, and it's gross out. Want to hit the pool?

I looked at Vivi. "Do you want to nap or go swimming?"

I asked her. This was one of the rare days I didn't have to be at the stable after school since we were easing into lessons this week.

She tapped her chin with a finger. "I could nap on a pool raft!"

"You're a genius, you know that?"

"I do, but thanks for confirming it." She stuck out her arms to me, and I took her hands and gently pulled her off the bed.

We changed into our bathing suits and grabbed a couple of towels, and I nabbed a tote from Vivi's closet to fill with bottled water, sunblock, and a few snacks. On our way out, I double-checked to make sure the door to Amherst was locked along with our room door, and we headed for the pool, our flip-flops slapping the sidewalk in a strangely calming way. Going to the pool would be a great way to relax before slipping into show-prep mode.

"How are you feeling about"—Vivi gestured around—"everything?"

"Good," I said. "Surprisingly good. Not going to lie, yesterday was a major blow to how safe and secure I felt here, but in a way, it fired me up even more to figure this out."

"It shook me, too," Vivi said. "Having anyone in your space who isn't supposed to be there is weird." She shuddered, even though it was in the low nineties outside.

"I'm sorry. I know it happened to you, too, and I've made this all about me."

"Oh my god, no," Vivi said, shaking her head. "Don't apologize at all. Yeah, it happened to me, but it wasn't directed at me. So, it's very different. All I want is to figure it out."

"Me too. And we will. We just have to be patient now and wait for them to make a move."

"Then we pounce," Vivi said, smiling.

"Exactly."

I smiled too, bumping my shoulder against hers. I kept having waves of guilt about not telling Vivi and Thea about the reason why the TXP made me so nervous. Maybe, maybe I needed to tell them. Somehow. Sometime. But not today. Definitely not until I got the first show of the season out of the way. I could only handle so much right now.

Together, we entered the pool area. It was a sea of red brick and palm trees with fairy lights that made the whole place feel like a tropical vacation spot. There were several patio tables with brightly colored oversized umbrellas, deck chairs, and lounge chairs. Vivi and I put our stuff on one of the pool-side tables and kicked off our flip-flops. It was wonderfully empty here now, but I was sure the pool would be teeming with people soon.

I shimmied out of my jean shorts and tugged off my T-shirt. We grabbed our towels and laid them out on two lounge chairs. Vivi looked over at my towel and shook her head.

"What?" I asked.

"I'm getting you a new one for Christmas," she said, laughing gently. "Abs, that one is falling apart!"

"Is not!" Okay, it totally was. "And besides, you can't just 'get me a new one.' It's my towel from my trip to—"

"Union, Connecticut," Vivi finished for me. "The birthplace of *the* Sasha Silver. The city that forever changed the world because it gave us Sasha." She grinned. "Did I get all that right?"

I couldn't help but smile. "You did. But see? Now you know why I can't get a new towel."

So what if my towel emblazoned with UNION across the center in a Gothic font was faded? And had a few bleached spots from the washing machine. And a raggedy corner. The green-and-gray towel was still one of my dearest possessions, and not just because of Sasha. It reminded me of the road trip Mom and Dad had taken me on far from home to see the birthplace of my idol. Lauren Towers had lived in Union too, of course, but she hadn't been born there like Sasha. So I always associated Union with Sasha.

It had been the last trip I'd ever taken with my mom. She'd been as excited to go as I'd been. Maybe more so because she'd known how big of a deal this trip was to me. It had been my surprise birthday present—a trip to Union. We'd rented an SUV, packed it up, and driven to Connecticut. Union was a small city—so there weren't actual tourist attractions. But nothing I wanted to see was on any big map, anyway.

We'd visited her old stable, Briar Creek, and had walked around the quaint and cheery downtown. I'd grown more and more in awe of Sasha with each stop we made. I'd imagined myself walking in her shoes and wondered if one day, someone would ever come to Fieldcrest and retrace my steps.

At the Union gift shop, I'd looked for a blanket, and they were out. So I'd taken a towel instead, and I'd stayed wrapped up in it the entire drive home. Technically, I could shop online and get a new one, but it wouldn't be the same as the one I had and loved.

"Cannonball!"

I snapped out of my memory, my head jerking toward the pool. I laughed as I watched Thea leap off the deck and wrap her arms around her legs. She was on the other side of the pool, and I'd been so lost in my thoughts, I hadn't even seen her get here.

She emerged from the water, wiping it from her eyes and grinning at me and Vivi. "Let's go! Get in!"

I looked at Vivi and held out a hand to her. "Ready?" I asked her.

She took my hand, nodding. "Ready!"

"CANNONBALL!" we yelled, jumping into the pool.

The cool water enveloped me, and I released Vivi's hand and let myself sink for a few seconds. Underwater, the noises around me were muffled and the sun's rays were muted. Kicking, I broke the surface and let out a contented sigh as a feeling of refreshment washed over me.

"Hello," Thea said, swimming over. "Fancy meeting you two here."

The three of us giggled.

"Total surprise to run into you," I said. "Are you stalking us or something?"

Thea waggled her dark eyebrows. "You know it."

Vivi swam to the edge of the pool and climbed the ladder. "Anyone want a pool noodle?"

I raised my hand, and so did Thea.

"Be right back," Vivi said.

"So, speaking of stalkers," Thea said. "Any updates?"

I filled her in. Vivi tossed each of us a pool noodle before jumping back in with her own. The three of us floated at the deep end of the pool, letting the sun warm our shoulders as we lazily kicked our feet.

"And Vivi told me she talked to Nina," I said. "And she doesn't know anything."

"Crap. Do you think she was telling the truth?"

I shrugged. "Vivi seemed to think so. She said Nina didn't appear to be lying, and she has an alibi for yesterday."

"Oh?"

"Yeah, she was in the common room at Charles House. Emery saw her there."

"I still wish we could tell someone," Vivi said. "An adult someone."

Thea gave us a sympathetic smile. "I wish you could too, but sadly, I think keeping it to yourselves is the right move."

Vivi groaned.

"For now," Thea added quickly. "If the TXP escalates in any way or breaks into your room again, then yeah, I'd tell your RA and I'd—"

With a wave of my hand, I cut Thea off mid-word. Behind her, Selly and Nina had walked into the pool area. They'd slowed down once they'd spotted us, and I didn't want them to overhear a single word Thea was about to say. Just in case.

Thea turned her head, spotting them and sighing.

"Definitely not the place to keep talking about that now," she said quietly.

"Nope," I said. I treaded the water harder as I tried to move more toward the center of the pool and away from the wall. "How are *you*, by the way?" I raised an eyebrow in Thea's direction. "All we've been talking about lately is me, ugh!"

"It's not your fault," Thea said. She gathered her long black hair into a high ponytail, securing it with an elastic from her wrist.

"But how are things?" Vivi asked. "I feel like we haven't gotten to see each other this week."

It made me so happy to see how close Vivi and Thea had become. I'd been the one to introduce them to each other last year. At first Thea had been solely my riding friend, until I'd started hanging with her outside of the stable. I'd guessed correctly that she and Vivi would like each other, and the two were now friends outside of their friendship with me. It made me feel powerful and a bit magical—like a friend matchmaker.

"Busy," Thea said. "The first week of school is always wild. But I'm hoping things start to settle down over the next couple of weeks."

"Same here," I said. "How's Cora? I think I saw her at the river party, but it was so full of people, I'm not sure."

"She's so excited to be here," Thea said. "I'm keeping an eye on her since she's new and everything. I really want this year to go well for her."

We kept talking as we floated in the pool. Nina and Selly, who had been whispering under one of the umbrellas, walked across the deck to the deep end. Selly glanced around as if she was checking to see if someone—anyone—was watching as she flipped her hair over her shoulder. Then she put her hands together above her head.

"It says 'no diving' only every foot around this pool," I said.

"And yet . . . ," Vivi said, tilting her head in Selly's direction.

Selly bounced on her toes and did a perfect dive into the pool. I glanced around to see if the on-duty lifeguard was going to blow his whistle and call her on it, but nope. Selly got away with *everything*. Always.

"C'mon, chicken," Selly said to Nina. "Are you getting in or not?"

Unlike Selly, Nina didn't dive in. She carefully slid into the water so she didn't splash Selly, which was ridiculous, since Selly was already in the pool.

"Want to get out and dry off?" I asked my friends. Suddenly, the pool wasn't enjoyable anymore.

Thea and Vivi nodded.

"Then dinner?" Thea asked. "We could grab fast food tonight instead of going to the cafeteria."

"I'm in," Vivi said. "I need fries. Or I shall simply perish." She put her forearm across her forehead.

Thea and I giggled.

"Perish, huh?" I asked. "That wouldn't be good."

Vivi's eyes were wide as she shook her head. "It wouldn't be."

Thea and I glanced at each other and cracked up.

"Well, come on then," I said, heading toward the shallow end of the pool. "Let's get you fries."

"They're always so loud and obnoxious." Selly's voice carried from the deep end of the pool. Nina was right next to her in the water, but Selly had raised her voice to make sure we heard her.

"Shhh," Vivi said, putting a finger over her lips as she spoke in an exaggerated whisper. "Guys, we're too loud."

"Oh!" Thea said loudly. "Right! Indoor voices at the outdoor pool."

I snorted. I loved my friends.

"Oh, Abby?" Selly called.

I turned back to face her, not saying a word. I quirked an eyebrow, waiting for her to speak first.

"Any luck figuring out who 'framed' you?" Selly asked, making giant air quotes.

"Yup," I lied. "We're getting close."

"Suure," Nina said, laughing. "Tell us! Who's on your suspect list?"

"C'mon," Thea said, tugging on my forearm. "Don't tell them anything. They're not worth it."

She was right, and I didn't want them to know how *not* close at all we were.

We climbed out of the pool and grabbed our towels,

deciding to dry as we walked instead of hanging around.

Selly's eyes flashed, following us as we left. I wanted to turn around and say something snarky, something biting, but I kept my mouth closed. Once we figured it out, we could rub it in their faces, but until then, I needed to keep all TXP theories to myself.

Friday Junior

B YE, GREEN FRIENDS," I SAID TO MY plants as Vivi and I headed out to breakfast on Thursday morning. "Make good choices!"

Vivi laughed. "I love your convos with them. Especially giving them advice when we leave."

I pressed a hand to my chest in mock horror. "It would be rude of me to leave without a word. I've done that before, gotten all the way onto the quad and realized it. It took everything in me not to run back and apologize to them."

Vivi laughed, smoothing her navy T-shirt. "You're a weirdo, you know that?"

I nodded. "Yup. Sure do."

"Don't ever change, 'kay?"

"Never."

And with that, we made a right and headed down the sidewalk toward the cafeteria. I crossed my fingers that I'd be able to focus enough to get by in class today and not be too distracted by tomorrow, aka show day.

In the caf, I grabbed an everything bagel, an OJ, and a dish of watermelon before heading to my usual table. Thea, Willa, and Ankita were already there—chatting away—and I sat down with a smile. Vivi took a seat across from me.

"It is finally Friday Junior, friends," Ankita said.

"Right?" I said. "I tried to tell Vivi that this morning." I shrugged. "She wasn't interested, though."

Vivi snorted. "It was early, oh my god. Abby was unusually chatty, and I wasn't even awake yet!"

Thea speared a piece of cantaloupe, nodding. "Well, it *is* known that you're not a morning person, V."

"See?" Vivi said, sticking out her tongue at me. "Sweet vindication for my response this morning!"

We all cracked up and dug into our breakfasts. The cafeteria was loud this morning—it seemed as though everyone was excited that the weekend was almost here.

"This is one time I wish I rode horses," Vivi said, shaking her head.

"What? Why?" Ankita asked.

Vivi pointed her fork at me and then at Thea. "Those two luckies don't have school tomorrow. So today's basically their Friday!"

"Ohh, right," Ankita said, her warm brown eyes on me. "Showtime, huh?"

I nodded. "Yup. First show of the season."

"And you ride for three entire days?" Ankita asked. "That sounds like a lot."

"Oh, no," I said. "It's three-day eventing, so we show once in each phase over those three days, and then we're done riding for the day—like, the show-jumping phase only takes a few minutes once we're mounted."

"But after we're done, we'll usually stick around and watch other riders or help our teammates," Thea added.

"There's a lot to learn by watching other riders," I said. "Not just our stable either, but area stables too."

"And we want to keep an eye on the competition by watch-ing other shows online," Thea said, "especially ones with—"

"Ava and Olivia," we said at the same time.

"Who are they?" Vivi asked.

"They're from Canterwood Crest," I explained.

"Ohhh," Vivi said. "That explains it, then."

"Yeah. Ava's a dressage queen, and Olivia is an all-around powerhouse," I said, rolling my eyes. "And Olivia is a Woolsworth, and she never lets anyone forget it."

Thea nodded. "Ever."

"What's a Woolsworth?" Ankita asked.

"Equestrian royalty. Her mom is a famous eventer, and her dad is a world-class trainer. He's trained US Olympic riders."

"We'll go up against them soon," Thea said. "And I'm *ready* for it."

"I really want to come watch sometime," Ankita said, sip-ping her steaming Earl Grey tea. "Let me know when the next show is, Abs. I want to see you and Thea ride and crush Ava and Olivia!"

Her enthusiasm made me smile. That level of support made me feel so grateful for our friendship.

"I'll text you the next competition dates," I promised.

"What's everyone else doing this weekend?" Thea asked as we ate.

"Absolutely nothing," Willa said. "I'm chilling on the couch with TV. I need a break after this week."

My other friends and I nodded. Going back to school after summer break was always painful.

"I'm going to the movies tomorrow with some people from theater," Vivi said. "But then, I'm with Willa—I don't want to do anything."

"Same," Ankita said. "Although, I'm going to meet with the debate team for pizza. We want to catch up after break and get ready for debate season."

"That sounds fun," I said. "I'd be a terrible debater, though."

Ankita shook her head, her dark hair flying. "No, you wouldn't! You should come to one of my debates this year. See what you think. You might be a future debater and not even know it yet."

"I definitely don't have debate in my future, but of course I'll come," I said.

"Are you all still going to the beach next weekend?" Ankita asked.

I nodded. We'd finally cemented the plan to go, and Maia

and one of the other older riders had agreed to take us. "I wish you rode horses," I said. "I feel bad that you can't come, but it would be no fun for you if we were all riding and you weren't."

Ankita waved a hand. "Omigosh, don't feel bad at all. Horses are terrifying, and I'm perfectly happy not climbing aboard one of those furry giants with enormous teeth, thank you very much."

I smiled. "Okay, you aren't wrong about them being furry giants with enormous teeth, but only if you're sure you don't want to come."

"I'm one million percent positive," Ankita said. "Plus, I've been kind of meh on the beach lately."

Everyone at our table stopped eating and stared at Ankita.

"What?" Vivi asked. "How can you be 'meh' about the beach?"

"This is brand-new information," Thea said. "You love the beach!"

Ankita laughed, shrugging one shoulder. "I know! I used to. But I'm digging the pool more lately. The beach feels . . . *questionable* to me. There's sand everywhere, it takes multiple showers to stop smelling like the ocean, and"— Ankita shivered—"do we really know everything that's swimming around in there? Don't you ever worry that some unknown, undiscovered sea creature is going to swim out of the depths and bite you?"

I put down my fork, giving Ankita my full attention. "You know, I was going to say no, and that I never have and never will worry about that. But now?" I grimaced. "I think I should?"

Thea nodded. "We definitely don't know everything that's in the ocean, that's for sure. I'd like to hope the odds of something—anything—biting me are low. But yikes, I do *not* like imagining what's in there that we don't know about yet!"

"Right?" Ankita said. "That's what I'm saying."

"The unknown is fascinating, though," Thea said. "What if there are merfolks thousands of feet below the surface?"

"Okay, Ariel," I said, laughing. "I wouldn't be opposed to it! As long as someone teaches me how to breathe underwater and takes me to explore a cool sunken ship."

"This isn't helping my imagination," Ankita said, giggling. She twisted one of the silver bangles on her wrist. "But you've definitely made me feel even more sure that sticking with the pool is the right decision."

I couldn't help but smile as I looked at my friends. I was lucky to have each of them, and spending breakfast chatting about sea creatures and being silly made me so happy.

We got up, heading our separate ways out of the cafeteria. But as I walked past one of the tables, I heard familiar grating laughter and tried not to turn in its direction.

"Abby!"

Sigh. I turned toward Selly, who was sitting across from Joss and Nina at their usual table. For someone who hated me, Selly sure tried to talk to me a lot.

"What?" I asked.

"I was just talking about you," Selly said, polishing an apple with her napkin like some kind of old-school Disney villain.

"Cool," I said. "Have fun with that!"

As much as I wanted to know what she'd been saying about me, I also didn't. At all.

"It wasn't anything bad, Abby," Selly said. "Actually, it's the opposite."

"Okay?" I hated that she'd piqued my interest, but she had.

Selly took a bite from her apple, chewing thoughtfully. "I'm worried about you."

"Yeah," Nina said, nodding. "Tomorrow is going to be tough."

I glanced back and forth between them. "Why?"

"It's your first show of the season," Selly said, giving me a sympathetic smile. "You're probably so worried after Fieldcrest."

"That would be enough to freak out anyone," Nina said.

"And on top of that, you've got Emery," Selly said, her tone so matter-of-fact.

I sighed, rolling my eyes. "You both really called me over here to tell me that? To try and psych me out about tomorrow?"

Selly's hand flew to her chest. "What? No, of course not. We're honestly concerned, Abs."

Abs? She'd never called me Abs. E-v-e-r.

"I know you're not worried," I said, shaking my head. "At all. This is textbook reverse psychology to try and make me worry about stuff I'm not even thinking about."

"You shouldn't repress those kinds of thoughts," Selly said. "They'll bubble up when you least expect it."

"I'm not repressing anything!" I said. "I've thought about Fieldcrest plenty, thank you. And I have no worries about Emery."

That last part wasn't entirely true, but I hoped she'd think it was.

"You don't have to lie to us," Nina said. "I'd be worried too about Emery joining our team and competing in our division. She's really good."

I stood up taller, pushing back my shoulders. "She is. And so am I."

And, with that, I walked away—leaving Selly, Nina, and Joss to "worry" on their own.

It's Go Time!

SHOW DAY NUMBER ONE DAWNED crisp and clear, and together, Thea and I climbed on the bus to the stable. Sleepily, we leaned against each other and sipped the black-tea-and-lemon drinks I'd grabbed from Sweets for us.

"This is so good, Abs. Thanks," Thea said.

"It really is. And you're welcome. I didn't want you drooling on my arm when you fell asleep on me from lack of caffeine."

"One time!" Thea said, groaning. "Once! I got the teensiest

spot of drool on your arm. But in my defense, we'd woken up at three thirty for a show and I was beat."

"I need to start wearing a raincoat to protect my arms," I teased. "Since we're going to be getting up early a lot this year."

Thea stuck out her tongue. "Totally worth it, though. I'll perk up once we get to the barn."

We'd gotten lucky for this show—Foxbury was hosting, so we wouldn't have to travel. It was going to be great for Beau to sleep in his own stall at night and for me not to have to pack us up to hit the road.

"I will too," I said. "Getting up early for school? Meh. Getting up early for a horse show? Okay!"

"That's the truth," Thea said. "Once I wake up in a few minutes, I'll be good to go. We are going to sweep this one, Abs. I have a feeling! I did a tarot card pull last night for each of us, and we both pulled good ones. Yours in particular."

Thea was into tarot readings and astrology, so she was forever pulling cards for us before big events.

"Ooh, really? Tell me! What did you pull?"

"I pulled the sun card for myself," Thea said. "That card stands for brightness, optimism, and joy. It's good luck and positive energy with a very sunny outcome!"

I grinned. "I love that for you, omigosh."

"And for you, I pulled the wheel of fortune card."

"What does that one mean?" I chewed on the inside of my cheek, anxious even though Thea had said it was a good card.

"It's a card associated with Jupiter, which is known as the planet of luck, so that's great," Thea said. "But it's also a card about destiny and fate. You don't know *exactly* what the universe has in store for you, but you have good luck coming your way."

"Today?"

Thea tilted her head. "Maybe? We don't know when it's coming with that card. But it *is* coming!"

"Hmm, well, I'm going to choose to believe that it means today! And if not today, then tomorrow or Sunday. As long as it happens this weekend, I'll be happy."

Thea raised her to-go cup to mine, and we tapped them together.

A short while later, we'd completed our horse inspection and turnout inspection, and it was almost time for my warm-up and then . . . my ride. I'd led Beau over to a quiet spot where we could watch the other dressage riders but still had some peace so I could relax a bit and get into the competitive mindset.

As team one's captain, Thea had pulled us all together for a last-minute pep talk, and it had left me feeling confident in the moment, but now my confidence was starting to wane and anxiety was on the verge of taking over.

"Thea pulled a good luck card for us," I told Beau as I wiped his nostrils and around his eyes with a soft cloth. "I hope it means we get the luck for this show."

Beau blinked at me, raising his head.

"I'm not saying we need luck, but it can't hurt."

But what if my practicing wasn't good enough? What if *I* wasn't good enough? I rubbed my forehead. *At least your dad has a shiny new daughter in case you mess up,* I thought. Emery's show record suggested she was plenty good. It made it all that much worse too that she was genuinely nice. I couldn't even hate her because she was a stuck-up jerk who was mean to everyone. I liked her even though I didn't want to.

Beau bumped his nose against my hip, almost as if he could hear my thoughts. He wasn't telepathic, but he sure could sense my moods.

"I don't want to lose my dad to Emery," I said in a whisper. "He's all I have."

Anger at my mom for ditching me simmered in my body.

None of this—from my worry about my dad to my insecurity toward Emery—would be happening right now if my mom had cared enough to stay.

Beau nuzzled my elbow, blowing gently through his nostrils. "You're right," I said. "I have you, too. I'm just . . . scared."

There were a lot of things I was scared of—and the biggest fears of all? Not achieving my dreams and losing my dad. More than anything, I wanted to be a superstar equestrian. I wanted to compete in college and, like Sasha Silver, be on track for the Olympics. Horses were my life, and there was nothing I wanted more than to do well in the competitive equestrian circuit.

But my desire to do well, my need to do well, were also fueled by my ever-present fear of abandonment. Even now, five years after my mom had walked out, I was left with so many questions. My biggest one: Had she left because of me? Because of something I hadn't been, or hadn't done, or wasn't?

I couldn't help but wonder what would happen if I made it to nationals this year. If I won at nationals and picked up a sponsorship, maybe my mom would see my face on a riding magazine. Or endorsing a horse product. Or even a lip gloss, like the company that had sponsored Sasha when she was in high school. Maybe Mom would see me and want to be my mom again. But did I really even want her back? After everything she had done, maybe I never wanted to see her again. Even though I thought I did. My feelings about Mom changed daily. Hourly, sometimes.

I looked out over the pasture, one of my favorite spots on the entire campus, as I tried to think about anything other than my mom. White oak fences went as far as my eye could see—stretching to the woods that flanked the back of the stable's campus. The ground sloped gently down to the stable, and riders were still working horses in the few outdoor arenas.

Beau nudged my arm again, and I petted his neck, stroking his soft coat. I let my fingers glide over his shoulder, feeling the familiar smoothness of his clean hair. He stood still as I finger-combed his mane, hoping to distract myself enough so I'd get out of my head.

"I want the top spot," I told Beau. "But how do I compete against them? They're *so* good."

Maybe Emery was going to crush me in the competition. Then it would be her and Selly at the top. How was I ever going to break through? Selly, as much as I couldn't stand her, was a fantastic rider. She was focused, driven, and not afraid of taking risks with her riding. She didn't get rattled. Like, ever. Her nerves of steel suited her well as a rider.

Emery was almost as good as Selly. With another year of training, she'd be better than Selly, I had a feeling. She had that magical "it" factor that other riders dreamed of having.

Beau lazily flicked an ear toward me, snorting.

I pushed my shoulders back, straightening a little. "You're right. They're good. But you know what? So are we. We can do this. We know our dressage test, and we are going to have a great ride. There. I am manifesting it, which is totally something Thea would say."

Beau nodded in agreement.

"All I can do is make myself proud," I said to Beau. "Then Dad will be proud of me too. Right, boy?"

Beau grunted, bobbing his head a bit. The sun peeked through some of the clouds and glinted off his deep bay coat. I loved horses of all colors, but I'd always had a special place in my heart for bays.

I checked my watch, and it was time to warm up. I could do this. I was *going* to do this. Blood raced through my veins, and the feeling made me stand taller. The thrill of competition was unlike anything else.

"Let's do this!" I told Beau.

Go Blue,
or Go Home

BEAU AND I WARMED UP, AND WHEN
the bell sounded, we had forty-five seconds to enter
the arena and begin our test. I took a deep breath
and trotted Beau through the entrance, where Thea stood
off to the side, giving me a thumbs-up. Nina and Thea had
already ridden and received fantastic scores, so now it was up
to me to finish off the dressage phase of the event for our team.

"Up now in ring two is Abigail St. Clair, riding Beau of
Mine," the announcer said.

I kept my gaze between Beau's ears and didn't allow myself

to look at the stands, which were packed with spectators. It would only make me nervous to see all the unfamiliar faces.

You can do this, I told myself as I halted Beau and saluted the judges. *You know this test, so show everyone.*

And so, we began.

We tracked left at a working trot, and Beau's gait felt smooth, and he was engaged in his movements. We turned into our first twenty-meter circle, and I felt Beau's body bend as it should while we made a circle.

With each move we made, Beau was eager to please and willing to do whatever I asked. I sat deeper in the saddle as we began to move from a working canter to a working trot, asking Beau to slow, and he made the transition calmly and with ease.

Since this was a dressage test, we needed to move from letter to letter across the arena, performing a specific movement at each letter.

On our way to C, he popped his head up a bit and I kept my hands quiet, sat deep in the saddle, and asked him to calm down and drop his head. Thankfully, he listened, and a wave of relief ran through me.

At C, we went into a medium walk and hit the halfway

point in our test, and the last few moves of the middle flew by. Beau was in tune with my every ask as we moved across the ring. His strides felt even, and his pace wasn't too fast or too slow.

I wished I could tell him how great he was doing, but I couldn't now. Not until after.

I asked him for a working canter as we went from C to M to B. His lines were straight, and he had a nice amount of bend when we took the corner, heading for F. I tried not to get excited and to stay focused, but this was one of our best tests. Ever. E-V-E-R! His movements felt like an extension of my body, and everything I asked for he gave to me with his very best.

At a working trot, we hit A and I took him down the centerline. *Almost done, you're almost done,* I thought. *Keep it together. Give a perfect halt.*

I eased him to a halt at X, transferring the reins to one hand so I could salute the judges. He didn't resist for a single second when I asked him to stop.

"And that was Abigail St. Clair on Beau of Mine, riding for Foxbury," the announcer said.

With that, I grinned and leaned forward in the saddle and

patted Beau's shoulder. "Way to go, boy! You were so perfect! I'm so, so proud of you!"

Beau was going to get so many carrots later! That ride was *magical*!

"Nice job, Abby!" someone called from the stands.

My head snapped up, and I looked to the stands and saw Natalie waving at me. I hadn't even seen her, since I'd refused to allow myself to look into the stands. I'd figured she'd been in the barn hanging with Emery while the other girl awaited her turn. But no, Natalie had been in the stands watching me. I couldn't help but smile and wave back.

I rode Beau out of the arena and dismounted. My feet were barely on the ground before Thea grabbed me in a hug.

"Omigod, what was that ride?!" she half yelled in my ear.

"I have no idea!" I said. "Beau was so, so good!" I hugged Thea, then wrapped my arms around Beau's neck to squeeze him.

"No, it wasn't just Beau," she said. "You both were fantastic. Abs, that was the best dressage test I've ever seen you do."

"I don't know what happened out there," I said, walking Beau forward. "But I'll take it. Dressage isn't our best phase by far, but wow, that felt good. He popped his head once. Once! Did you see that?"

"I did. He lowered it so fast, though. You didn't even react to it, and he was like, 'Okay, okay, I'll chill.'"

Thea stayed with me, waiting to get my dressage test score. And when it came in, we both shrieked. I stared at it hard, sure I wasn't really seeing such beautiful numbers in front of me. But I was!

DRESSAGE TEST SCORES FOR MIDDLE NOVICE:

ST. CLAIR, ABIGAIL: 67.1667 (32.83)

"I'm going into jumping with only 32.83 points," I squealed. "That's my personal best!" I said, dancing in place at the percentage. It would give me a low number of penalty points going into tomorrow, which was exactly what I wanted. And that, along with the jumping and cross-country scores, combined with my team's mount management score, would give me my total at the end of the show.

I loved that my rides were scored solo, but that as a team we got scored on equine management. It was an area I never had any problems with, so my marks were usually excellent.

"You totally deserve it," Thea said. "We're going to be in great shape going into tomorrow. I mean, Selly and Emery still have to ride, but Keir's ridden, and our team is done for the day. We can officially relax."

"That sounds so good," I said. "Once I'm finished with Beau and he's back in his stall, I want to catch Emery's ride. I'll miss Selly's, but I can make Emery's."

"Good plan," Thea said. "I'm going to go check on Nina, but I'm sure I'll run into you later."

As I began to cool out Beau, I crossed my fingers that Selly and Emery would do well—but that I'd keep my good placement. My test had put me in second place just behind Thea, and I wanted to hold steady even though there were still riders from other stables to go too, in addition to Selly and Emery. But Thea had been right—the pressure was off our team for today, and now I could sit back and enjoy the rest of the day.

Fool Me Once...

AFTER BEAU WAS BACK IN HIS STALL with his hay net and a fresh bucket of water, I patted his neck. "I'll see you later, boy. I'm going to go watch some rides."

I started out of his stall but froze when I heard what sounded like very angry feet stomping down the stable aisle.

"Are you kidding me?" Selly whined. "I'm in fourth. Fourth!"

"It's only the first phase," Nina said, her tone soothing. "There're two more to go. I know you'll catch up."

Selly sighed. "Thea, I get. She's a good dressage rider. But why is *Abby* ahead of me?"

"Abby got lucky. She won't do well at cross-country. You know she's gonna choke again."

"I hope so," Selly said.

I shook my head, staying silent inside Beau's stall until I was sure they were far away. Then I slipped out and hurried out of the stable. I could have confronted Selly about what she'd said, but it wasn't worth it. She wasn't worth it. But so much for team spirit from Selly. I laughed to myself. Hadn't she told Emery at lessons that she was the biggest cheerleader on the team?

Back near ring two, I spotted Emery finishing her warm-up on Bliss. She looked professional and show-ready in her white breeches and black riding coat, which looked much like mine.

Natalie was off to the side watching from the ground, a smile on her face as she looked at Emery. Maybe she was too nervous to sit in the stands. I felt that way watching my friends sometimes. I wanted to be as close to them as allowed while they were riding, and the stands could feel so far away.

For a second, I felt a stab of envy as I watched Emery wave to Natalie, mouthing something to her. *Your dad will be here tomorrow*, I reminded myself. *And then he'll be cheering you on.* I couldn't wait for him to come. It was going to be the best having him watch me ride.

The bell sounded, and Emery and Bliss were up.

"Now we have Emery Flynn riding her mare, Fanciful Bliss," the announcer said.

The chestnut mare trotted easily down the center and halted squarely with all four hooves perfectly placed. Emery gave a crisp salute to the judges, and even from my spot over here, I could see her slip into Professional Rider Mode. I held my breath as their test began, and Bliss moved with almost lyrical precision from letter to letter. Bliss's speed was great, and she moved with a fluid rhythm around the arena.

Then they went into a twenty-meter circle, and it wasn't as well-balanced as it could have been—the shape of the circle was lopsided. Emery stiffened up and lost some of her elasticity, bouncing a bit in the saddle. But they came out of the circle and started to canter, and Emery seemed to regain her awareness of how off her body had been. She relaxed, and I could see the suppleness come back in her thighs, her legs steady now.

I lost myself in her ride, listening to the rhythmic pounding of Bliss's hooves on the arena dirt. The mare was smaller and more compact than Beau, her strides a bit shorter. But she had powerful hindquarters that propelled her forward, and each hoof struck the dirt with exactness.

My phone buzzed in my hand, and I forced myself to tear my eyes away from the arena to look at the screen.

My mouth went dry at what I saw: a new text from an unknown sender.

The TXP.

Unknown sender: Isn't Emery's ride going well? She's so talented, right? And smart. I mean, she'd have to be. She's had you fooled!

I stared at the screen as if willing it to tell me who was behind this.

What did that mean? How did Emery have me fooled? It was probably nonsense—the TXP was trying to get me to worry. But why would they say this? *Think, Abby,* I told myself. What if this was how they wanted to pay me back for the whiteboard? Trying to make me turn on Emery and think something was wrong between us?

I put my phone facedown in my lap and scanned the arena, looking for anyone else on their phones. Anyone else who could be texting me. But that was impossible to tell—so many people were on their phones.

I texted Thea, but she didn't reply. She was probably super busy with team captain duties, ugh.

I didn't know what to do, so I sat there unmoving. Frozen. Emery finished her ride, and I clapped half-heartedly after she saluted. I hurried out of the stands, walking back to the stable.

Something was up.

Something was wrong.

My gut told me I had to talk to Emery about the text. I weaved around a couple of horses and riders, barely even seeing them since I was so lost in thought. *You're jumping to awful conclusions,* I told myself. *The TXP sent you that text to try and put another wedge between you and Emery. It's probably so fake.*

I hoped that was the case. That I was wrong, and I'd talk to Emery, and she would reassure me that she knew absolutely nothing about the text and had no possible idea what it could mean. Taking a breath, I headed for Bliss's stall and waited for Emery. I felt terrible ambushing her at a show, but our rides were finished for today. If I didn't talk to her now, I'd wonder about it until I did.

After I talked to her and she reassured me that I was totally and completely wrong and the TXP was lying, I would go walk the cross-country course. First, though, I had to do this.

Several long moments later, she and Bliss came down the aisle. Emery smiled when she saw me, giving me a small wave. I tried to smile back, but I couldn't. I was too anxious to find out what the text meant. Or didn't mean.

"Hey," Emery said slowly, her brow wrinkling. "What's up?"

I straightened, taking a deep breath. "Can we talk?" I blurted out.

Truth Exposed

MERY HESITATED, THEN NODDED. "Want to walk with me while I cool down Bliss?"

"Sure."

Emery pulled off her helmet and her jacket, then placed them on top of her tack trunk. "Is everything okay?" she asked.

I opened and closed my mouth, wordlessly shrugging. Finally, I said, "I'm not sure."

"Oookaay," Emery said. "You're kind of scaring me."

Together, we walked Bliss out of the stable and down toward one of the shaded lanes we used to cool out the horses. At least it was fairly private out here and away from the busyness of the heart of the grounds for us to talk. A few riders from other stables walked their horses up and down the lane, the sun glinting off their beautiful coats.

But I couldn't even enjoy looking at them. I was too panicked. My mind raced as we walked, and I tried to think about how to say what I needed to without hurting Emery's feelings. *She believes you about the faked video,* I reminded myself. *So show her the same courtesy.* Still, it felt like there was no right way to ask her about what the TXP meant.

"This is so awkward, but I got a text from the Truth X. Poser while you were riding," I said. "I know it's fake. I'm sure it is, honestly. But I wanted to talk to you about it. They're just trying to get in between us again, but I wanted you to know."

"What did the text say?" Emery asked, looking straight ahead as if she were focused on a point in the distance.

"Here." I unlocked my phone, clicked on the message, and held it up so she could see it.

She read it, and I watched her skin turn white in a way I'd only thought possible in cartoons.

"Abby," she started. She halted Bliss, coming to stand

directly in front of me. "I'm so sorry." Emery's voice was thick with tears, and the sounds of the show happening all around us faded away as I looked at her.

"What?" I asked. "Oh god. Please don't tell me that you secretly hate me. And that's what the TXP knows. Because"—I hesitated—"that would hurt. A lot."

She shook her head. "No, god."

"I know things haven't been perfect between us, but I didn't think you hated me or anything."

"I don't! Abby, that's not it."

"Then what? What is the TXP talking about?"

Emery licked her bottom lip, and a big tear rolled down her cheek. She swiped it away with her hand, taking a shaky breath. "I don't even know how to tell you this."

No. No. No.

This was *not* happening.

"No," I said. "No. Emery, tell me you're not . . . *them*. Tell me you're not the freaking Truth X. Poser!"

"I'm not! You got that text while I was riding, anyway!"

"Someone else could have had the phone and sent it for you." I stared at her. "Then what were you going to tell me?"

Emery's eyes flicked from me to an older boy who had

stopped his horse nearby while he fixed one of the horse's leg wraps. He was within earshot to hear our entire convo.

Finally, she looked back at me. "I'm so sorry, Abby. I know who it is. But you have to believe me, I tried to stop them! I swear!"

Bliss jerked her head into the air, snorting as she took a step back from Emery. The mare didn't want us to be having this conversation any more than I did.

I shook my head, trying to process what I'd just heard. "Are you kidding me, Emery? How could you know who it is and not say anything to me? That's practically just as bad! You've seen what they've been doing to me!" I couldn't stop yelling. I knew I shouldn't be this loud on stable grounds, especially when a show was happening on the other side of the lawn, but I couldn't seem to stop. "Who is it? Tell me!"

Out of the corner of my eye, I saw other riders staring at us as they walked their horses past us. If Rebecca heard about this, we were toast.

"Abby, let me explain, please. I didn't—"

"Who. Is. It?" I could barely even see straight. Tears clouded my vision, and I was so angry and hurt, it made me shake. For a second, I thought I might crumple to the ground.

"It's Nina. I wanted to be her friend!" Her words tumbled out faster and faster. "She told me you'd done something to Selly, and she wanted to get you back. I don't know what I thought she'd do, but it wasn't *that*."

It felt like I'd been punched in the stomach. I sucked in a breath, trying not to cry. Or scream.

"You knew Nina was coming after me?" I asked, every word slow and deliberate. "And you said *nothing*?"

Emery's mouth opened and closed. "I tried—I tried to get her to stop. Once I knew she was doing the TXP stuff. But she wouldn't, and I—"

"What I did to Selly was an accident!" I screeched. "What Nina did to me was on purpose, Emery!"

Suddenly, everything made sense now. My talk with Emery by the fountain came flooding back. She'd said she wanted me to stop digging because of how busy I was. No, it had been because she hadn't wanted me to find the truth with a giant arrow pointing in her direction and that she was covering for Nina.

"Did she try and convince you the video was real? Or did you know it was fake the entire time?"

"The day I asked you to meet me after school, I'd confronted Nina. I told her I didn't believe the video could be real. Not after you and I talked about it." Emery shook her head. "She practically laughed at me and told me of course it was fake."

"So, that day we went riding together, you didn't know?"

"No, I swear!"

I took a deep breath, trying to calm down as I watched Bliss's eyes widen and her nostrils flare. I tried to lower my voice, so I'd stop scaring her. "How did you even find out it was Nina?"

"She and I started talking more because we both live in Charles. One night we were hanging out, and she told me that she was such a loyal friend to Selly, and she'd be a good friend to me, too. I asked her what that even meant, and she told me she was just looking out for Selly and making someone else pay. Then you started getting harassed, and I put it all together."

Another memory came back. I'd texted Emery a pic of the whiteboard and had said something about how I had to get my suspect list narrowed down. And later, after someone had been in our room and keyed the X on the whiteboard, she'd told me I could take Nina off the list, since Nina had been in the Charles House common room when it happened.

"I let Nina off the hook for all of this because you gave her an alibi," I said. "You said she was with you when my white-board got destroyed. That was clearly a lie, wasn't it?"

"I—I just wanted you to stop looking. I thought if you hit a dead end, you'd give up and all of this would go away."

We both turned, startled, when Keir, leading Magic, came over to us. His eyebrows were up, and he approached us as if we were a flighty, nervous horse he wanted to calm down.

"Is everything . . . you know, *okay* over here?" he asked.

I glared at Emery, not saying a word.

"Everything's fine," Emery finally said, patting Bliss's neck.

"You sure?" he asked, glancing between us. "Abs?"

"Yeah, sorry," I said. "We're almost done."

"Okay," Keir said with a lingering glance as he eased Magic forward. "Come find me if you need anything."

Emery and I nodded, and I waited until he was out of earshot to ask, "How did Nina get into Amherst, Emery?" Something in my gut told me she knew.

She shifted, trying to keep Bliss close as the mare was getting jittery from standing by and watching and listening to us argue.

"She stole Selly's key and made a copy. Selly doesn't know."

"And she told you this? Wow. You two must be way closer than I thought." I couldn't keep the disgust out of my tone. "I tried with you, I really did. To be nice to you and be a friend. But do you think any of this has been easy on me? Moving into *your* house with *your* mom? Well, it hasn't been! It's sucked, in case you haven't noticed!"

"I know. You ha—"

"Don't. Don't pretend that you know anything about what it's been like for me. Your mom is amazing." The words tumbled out. "She's here to cheer you on and support you. Mine can't even be bothered to tell me where she lives."

Emery's lower lip trembled. "I'm sorry. That's not okay at all."

"No, it's not. And you know what the worst part is? Sometimes, I still want her to come back. Like nothing ever happened, and we'll go back to the way things used to be. How messed up is that?"

"It's not. She's your mom. No matter what. But things can't go back. My mom . . . really loves your dad."

I laughed bitterly. "Yeah. I know. Honestly, this isn't even about your mom. Or mine. This is about you." I folded my arms. "You could have told me the truth." I tried to keep my own voice from shaking. "God, all this time I've been trying to figure it out to prove to you that I didn't say any of those things about you or your mom, and you already knew! That's beyond messed up."

"I know, I know," Emery said, rubbing her red nose. "I'm so sorry, Abby. I should have told you. I wanted to, but I was scared."

"I've given you zero reason to be afraid to tell me. I've done exactly what my dad wanted—tried to be nothing but a friend to you." I took a breath, then spat out, "Even if I hated every second of it."

Emery's head jerked back as if I'd slapped her, and her eyes welled up with tears. For a split second, I thought about taking back the lie, but I was too hurt. Too angry.

"You—you didn't want to hang out with me?"

"No," I lied. "Not for a minute."

"Oh." She swiped at the tears on her cheeks. "Abby, I didn't—"

I snorted. "Just stop. You don't need me. You get to see my dad on FaceTime every week, remember? You're good."

"Wait, wait. He's only doing it with me because we barely know each other, and he doesn't think I'll reach out to him on my own. You will! He's your dad, and you—"

I shook my head, stepping away from her and Bliss. As I did, a group of three older riders who had stopped to listen to us argue pulled their horses away as they started back down the path. "Save it. I don't want to hear your excuses or 'reasons.' We're done. Don't *ever* speak to me again."

And with that, I turned on my heel, heading back down the lane.

"Abby, wait, please," Emery called after me, her voice breaking.

But I didn't turn back. Tears blurred my vision as I broke into a run. I had to get away from Emery.

Away from all of it.

Acknowledgments

Josh Getzler, never once did you make me feel like I was a burden of a client when I couldn't write anything. You stuck with me and didn't push too hard. And look at us now! Cheers to many, many more books together. Thank you for believing in me. And thank you to everyone at HG Literary, including the kind and helpful Jonathan Cobb.

Aly Heller, I'm so thrilled I get to do this again with you! Working with you is comfortable and easy—you make this whole process fun. Thank you for all your enthusiasm and support and for giving me this chance.

It's so fantastic to have another horse girl on these books, and it's been so great working with you, Jessi Smith!

Thank you to everyone at Simon & Schuster who is on Team Saddlehill and worked on my book, including Valerie Shea, Chel Morgan, Olivia Ritchie, Kaitlyn San Miguel, Karin Paprocki, Mike Rosamilia, Sara Berko, Valerie Garfield, Kristin Gilson, Anna Jarzab, Alissa Nigro, and Nicole Russo.

Lana Dudarenko, you gave me the cover of my dreams. Thank you!

Endless thank-yous to my reader turned dear friend, emily e dickson. I'll never forget calling you to share the news about these books, and I couldn't ask for a more supportive friend.

Marissa Eller, I'm so glad we met in Nashville! You're a true star in the writing community, and I can't wait to support the heck out of your future books.

Natalie Keller Reinert, Mary Pagones, and Megan Scott Molin—thank you for the support, from one equestrian to another, and for answering any horse-related questions. And so much thanks to the United States Pony Clubs and the Inter-scholastic Equestrian Association for providing such fantastic programs for young riders.

Teachers, booksellers, and librarians—y'all are heroes! Thank you for helping to get my books—and all the wonderful books out there—into the hands of readers.

Mary Kole, thank you so much for giving me a safe space to land and helping me get my groove back.

Thank you, Tess Sharpe, for all the encouragement and wisdom. And hugs to everyone in the Trifecta!

Rhona Gray, I wish you were here. I miss you.

Thank you so much to my parents and Jason for all the support and help while I was healing. And for all the encouragement when I started writing again. I'm very grateful for all you've done! And, Grandma, I told you I'm gonna write ninety books! Here's number twenty-seven!

Shanna Alderliesten, thank you so, so much for reading the early drafts and making sure all my horse scenes are on point. And thank you for both cheering me on and reminding me when I need to take a break. I adore you, and I'm so glad we're friends!

Misty Wilson, I'd be absolutely lost without you! There's no one else I'd rather send five hundred DMs a day to about everything and nothing. You've motivated me so freaking much, and I am so glad we found each other to be anxious messes with.

Julia Hezel, I am emotional at this moment, thinking about how close you came to not being around. I can't imagine going through life without you, and you are such a bright light in my life. I cannot thank you enough for all the cheerleading, love, and support you give me on the daily.

Jen Kurtyak, from the moment I said I was going back to writing, your only question was "How's it going today?" You never once doubted me or acted surprised when I succeeded after my string of failures and false starts. You made me believe I could write again and cheered me on daily whether I wrote one or one thousand words. And thank you, Lauren, for being just as excited and proud.

Finally, when I said I didn't think I'd be here, let alone releasing another book, I meant it. I had to hit rock bottom and lose everything to start to fight to get my life back. But I'm here, and I'm doing the thing. I'm so grateful and excited to share new stories with everyone. Thank you so much to my readers who have always, always had my back. I thank my lucky stars every day for you, and to my longtime Harts, I hope you enjoy all the Canterwood Crest mentions and Easter eggs. I sprinkled them in with y'all in mind! There's so much more to come!

DON'T MISS THE NEXT BOOK IN THE
SADDLEHILL ACADEMY SERIES!

Saddlehill Academy

THE SHOWDOWN

JESSICA BURKHART

FIVE GIRLS. ONE ACADEMY. AND SOME SERIOUS DRAMA.

CANTERWOOD CREST

by Jessica Burkhart

TAKE THE REINS
BOOK 1

CHASING BLUE
BOOK 2

BEHIND THE BIT
BOOK 3

TRIPLE FAULT
BOOK 4

BEST ENEMIES
BOOK 5

LITTLE WHITE LIES
BOOK 6

RIVAL REVENGE
BOOK 7

HOME SWEET DRAMA
BOOK 8

CITY SECRETS
BOOK 9

ELITE AMBITION
BOOK 10

**SCANDALS,
RUMORS, LIES**
BOOK 11

**UNFRIENDLY
COMPETITION**
BOOK 12

CHOSEN:
SUPER SPECIAL

INITIATION
BOOK 13

POPULAR
BOOK 14

COMEBACK
BOOK 15

MASQUERADE
BOOK 16

JEALOUSY
BOOK 17

FAMOUS
BOOK 18

HOME FOR CHRISTMAS:
SUPER SPECIAL

READ&
LEARN

with

simon kids

75458

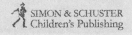

SIMON & SCHUSTER
Children's Publishing

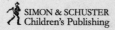